Chronicles of
Myriad
Quest for the Oracle

James Nicholas Adams

ISBN: 978-1-958626-80-1
Library of Congress Control Number: 2024901425

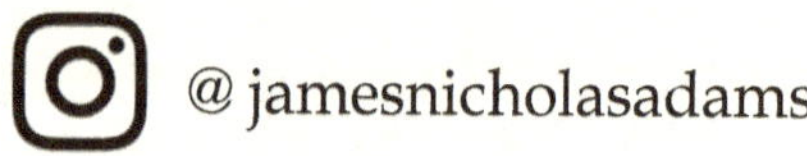

https://www.jamesnicholasadams.com

Cover design by Brad Lund.
Copyright © 2021

To my loving wife Mary who has
supported me every step of the way.

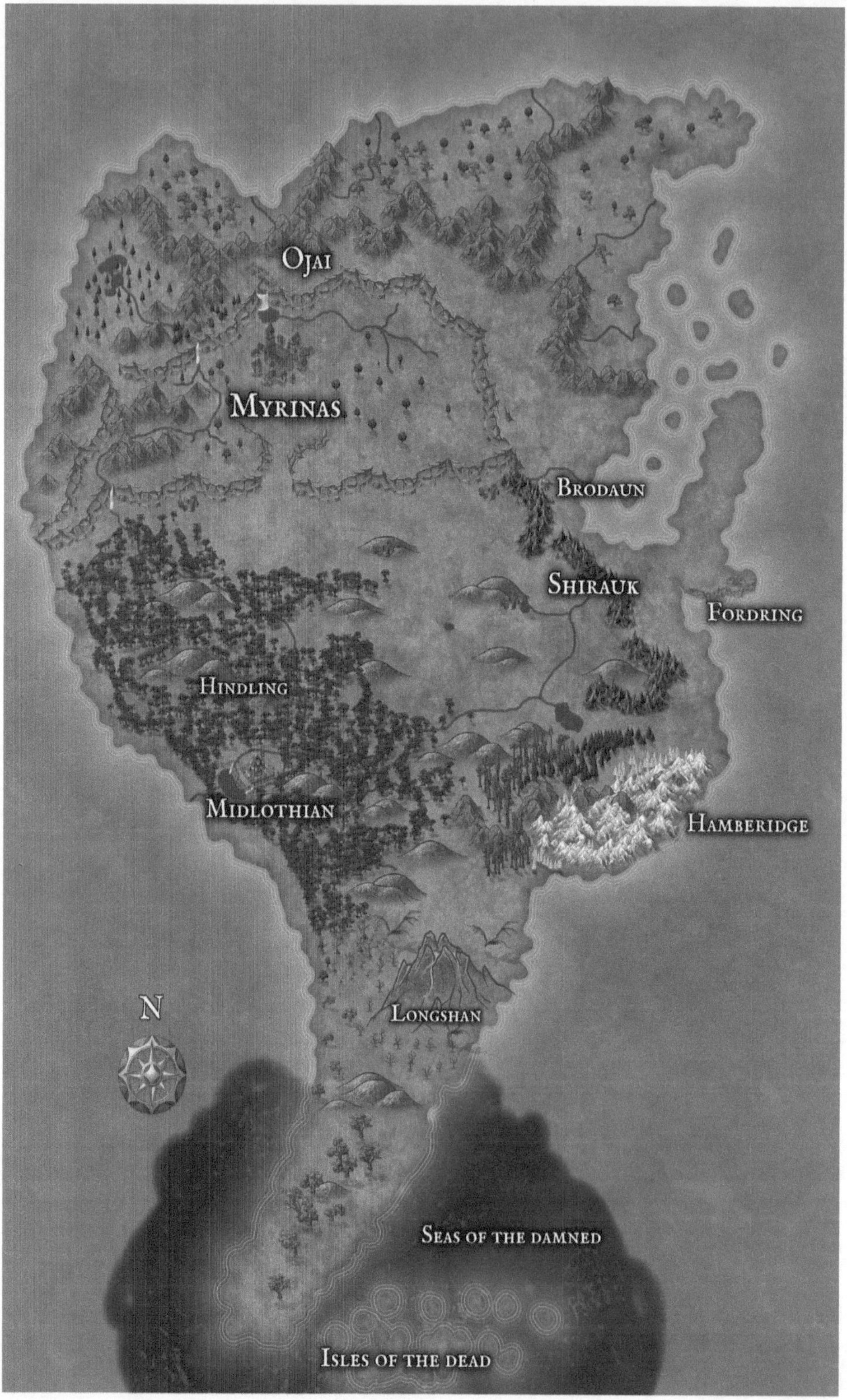

Ojai
Myrinas
Brodaun
Shirauk
Fordring
Hindling
Midlothian
Hamberidge
N
Longshan
Seas of the damned
Isles of the dead

"Quest for the Oracle feels like a bedtime story.
It takes familiar fantasy elements and presents
them in new ways, engaging the reader
with the captivating story."

"As a parent, it's such a relief to find a wholesome
and entertaining book that you actually want
your child to get lost in and that's exactly what
this book is."

"An absolute feast for the imagination."

Contents

A lot of the character names in Chronicles of Myriad can be said how they look. For some of the trickier ones, here is a guide to help.

Akarah	AH car uh
Aris	AH riss
Baidel	Bye dell
Ojai	OH jeye
Silamond	Sil uh mahnd
Tanas	Tah nahs
Naiev	Neye ehv
Jerech	Jair eck
Gaibian	Guy b en
Bahamut	Buh ha mutt
Kaelthith	Kay el thith
Draedin	Dray din
Othniel	AH the nell
Dalatori	Dall uh tor ee
Raltiiri	Ral tear ee
Raza	Raw zuh

Prologue

Best of Friends

Daniel England had just finished medical school in New York when it was discovered that his wife Carolyn was unable to have children. Devastated by this news, Carolyn expressed her desire to leave New York for a more peaceful life. On November ninth of nineteen hundred ninety that they moved into their home in Keash, Ireland where Daniel opened up a small medical office.

Their luck, however, had not completely run out. Just seven months after their arrival came the welcome gift of a baby boy. A blonde-haired, amber eyed boy named Jason.

Jason was introduced to the girl that became his best friend; the daughter of Johnathan and Kiera Simmons, Kristine. Kristine was a beautiful girl with long black hair and piercing emerald eyes. Daniel and Carolyn became very close friends with Johnathan and Kiera when they moved to Ireland, so it was only natural for their children to grow up together. Jason and Kristine were friends instantly and were hardly ever apart. That is, until Kristine's twelfth birthday.

Like every other one of her birthdays, Jason woke up early and ran over to Kristine's as fast as he could. He stopped under her window and shouted at the top of his lungs, "Happy Birthday Kristine!!!" He waited anxiously for her window to open. Nothing happened. He sucked in a deep breath and yelled even louder, "Wake up, sleepy head! It's your birthday!" Still no answer.

He walked to the door and pulled his fist back to knock. The door slowly creaked open by a passing breeze. Jason walked in and looked around. The living room was empty. He rushed up the stairs to Kristine's room. Empty. Room after room he searched in a panic, calling her name. It seemed the house had been abandoned.

He quelled his discouragement and thought aloud, "I know where she is!"

He left the abandoned house – a thick fog had filled the air. He began running as fast as his legs would carry him. Without stopping he climbed to the top of the steep hill that led to the Keash caves. When he reached the caves he began calling her name again. The sound echoed as he yelled into one after the other. All empty. He kicked the dirt in frustration then dropped to his knees. A glimmer on the ground in the early morning sun caught Jason's eye. He reached down and picked it up. A tree encircled by interwoven branches and roots meeting together in the middle held a semi-transparent opal sphere. Various colors glistened inside as the light hit it. Jason recognized the pendant he had bought for Kristine's last birthday. Jason slipped it around his neck and walked slowly home.

"Jason! Thank God you're alright! You know we don't like you wandering around when its foggy like this." Carolyn wrapped her arms around Jason who now had tears falling down his cheeks. Carolyn wiped the tears from her boy's eyes, "What's wrong, sweetie?"

"She's gone," Jason sniffed.

"Who's gone honey?"

"Kristine. She left and didn't say goodbye."

Just then Daniel walked into the room, "What's going on?"

Carolyn looked up at her husband, "Jason seems to have lost his imaginary friend."

Jason tried again and again to make his parents see the light but it seemed they had no recollection of Johnathan and Kiera Simmons or their daughter. By all appearances, they never existed anywhere but in Jason's young mind.

He could never understand how his parents denied her existence. Time after time Jason insisted they had met her. What was more they had been friends with her parents. The young boy grew more distraught with each passing year. Daniel and Carolyn felt their quiet life in England had come to an end. Shortly after Jason turned twelve, the Englands picked up and moved to Mount Angel, Oregon. Even here, Jason felt empty without Kristine.

Yet as much as he argued it, it always ended the same way; his parents would look him in the eye and say, "She was just your imagination." Finally Jason gave up and never brought Kristine up to his parents again. This, however, was not a sad ending. In fact it was not an ending at all; this was only the beginning.

1

The Prophecy

Hatred built up for many years in the hearts of the proud Dragons; hatred towards the vile beings that deceived and enslaved them. The Angels had promised freedom to the Dragons from the humans that hunted and killed them on Earth. A promise was given that they would live freely on a planet in the farthest reaches of the universe. In trust, the Dragons followed the seven children of Ojai, the first of the Angels. Upon reaching the magnificent planet the Dragons were immediately chained and forced to construct a great city for their dying mother Naiev.

Being the largest and strongest Dragon, beside his father Bahamut, Kaelthith was kept separate from the rest. Four chains were clamped tight around his long scaly neck and anchored deep in the rocks. A larger clamp was secured around his black body and leathery wings. His long, spike-tipped tail was locked directly to the ground. Four chains bolted to the rock stretched to clasps attached to each of the dragon's legs giving him barely enough slack to lay his body on the hard ground.

Anger and hatred was deeply rooted in the heart of the young prince of the Dragons, deeper than any living creature had ever felt, consuming his soul. One night in his dreams, Kaelthith was visited by a cloaked figure who introduced himself as Draedin. Draedin swore the dragons would be freed from the Angels and revenge could be had upon the deceitful race.

"What must I do," the Dragon prince hissed into the dark.

"You are a wise and powerful leader, my young friend. Swear your loyalties to the eternal Dark Alliance and I will grant you greater power than you have ever imagined. Your people will be free."

Kaelthith's enormous form stood before the hooded man. A demonic hand reached into the Draedin's cloak and pulled out a silver dagger. He gestured for Kaelthith to bow down. The dragon's head lowered and he closed his eyes solemnly. A sharp line stretch across Kaelthith's forehead then he felt the dagger cut deep, curving lines outward over his eyes. "This is the sign of your power and loyalty," Draedin said.

As the warm blood trickled down his face to the feet of the shrouded figure Kaelthith echoed the oath spoken to him, "By the royal blood that flows through my veins and by the power passed to me from my forefathers, I swear the allegiance of myself and my race to the great Lord Draedin. I swear an oath to seek vengeance on all the enemies of the Dark Alliance, that my Lord may, too, be free from the bonds that tie him."

The blood soaked into the thirsty earth. A sinister laugh escaped from the unseen face beneath the hood of the black cloak.

The large black Dragon woke from his dream. With cold, red eyes he searched the darkness about him. He growled lowly through a mouthful of razor sharp teeth as he felt the pain on his face. Black blood dripped on the ground below him.

The pain started as a pin prick at the tip of

Kaelthith's tail and flowed quickly through his body as every vein inside him began to boil. A loud, pained roar erupted out of the Dragons throat, spreading through the nearly completed Angelic City. All around, Kaelthith's race struggled to see what was happening to their Prince. His body writhed on the ground as an unseen force tortured him. Kaelthith's body began to change dramatically. His body shrank causing the chains to rattle as they fell to the ground. What was once an enormous Dragon transformed, limb by limb into an almost human form. Kaelthith now knelt, holding his chest with a clawed hand, and steadied his breathing. Though the rough skin, long tail, and leathery wings resembled that of a smaller dragon, the prince had become something entirely different. Inside the dark prince's mind, Draedin spoke to him, and gave him the words to offer to his astonished watchers.

"My kin, the time has come for the great Dragons to evolve into an even greater race. Our time of freedom has at last been delivered because of the leadership of your prince. Swear your loyalty to me and you shall all be free."

One by one the dragons bowed their head in compliance to the prince's command. As they did, each changed in the same manner as Kaelthith. They knelt before their great leader and listened intently to the instruction given to them.

"The time of the Dragons has ended and given birth to the far greater and more powerful Daedra." Kaelthith turned, "Follow me to the place we shall make our home, away from the eyes of the deceiving Angels."

As they were about to take flight, two Angelic guards arrived to find out what had caused the entire city to wake.

"What's going on here?" the one of the guards demanded, "Who are you and what have you done with the Dragons?"

The crowd parted as Kaelthith turned walked back toward the two warriors. "You are fools for coming here. We are the Dragons. We are your former slaves and the future end of your wicked race."

Kaelthith's clawed hand wrapped around the neck of the Angel that spoke to him. His grip tightened, and blood began to seep through Kaelthith's fingers. The silver blood of the Angel began to burn Kaelthith's hand, causing him to drop the guard to the ground. Kaelthith turned to face his people, as if he would address them once more. In one swift motion, the Daedra's tail flew down driving one of the spikes through the guard's head, killing him.

Kaelthith cocked his head to the side and spoke to the frightened Angel still remaining, "Run away, boy, and tell your king his time will soon come to an end."

Kaelthith watched as the other sentry turned and flew quickly back toward the magnificent city before he rose to the sky. Following in step with their prince, each Daedra spread their leathery wings and took off into the night from the high plateau putting distance between themselves and their enslavement.

* * *

Nearly two hundred years passed since the Daedra escaped captivity. The Angels were devastated that night by the murder of their father as well. Ojai's wish to have his youngest son Baidel take the throne was fulfilled. He forbade the use of slaves and gave the order that the Angel's would watch over and protect the humans as penance.

Rumors soon reached the ears of Aris, the young prince of the Angels, that an army was massing in the south with the sole purpose of completely eradicating the Angels from existence. Against his father's wishes, Aris began preparing an army for invasion. They trained hard, both day and night. The days turned into weeks, weeks to months, and months to years, and still there was no attack on the city.

As tension heightened and rumors of mutiny began to spread, the skies grew darker. Clouds slowly moved in from the south, covering the lands. At last the army began to break apart until Aris stood alone in the keep. Aris left the city, and disguised himself as a human, spending much of his time at a pub inside Myrinas, hoping to hear of any strange dealings nearby. He allied himself with the Elves of the Dark Woods, befriending the king. He asked them to keep their keen eyes open for signs of an army moving through the woods - or the sky.

As The War of the Races began, the Angels diverted their attention back to the protection of the humans in the city at the base of the mountain. Myrinas became the site of much death and destruction. Reconstruction of the city took over a hundred years. Improvements were made in the city's defenses, and the borders were expanded. Aris began, once again, seeking signs of the nearly forgotten threat against his people. Again, he began visiting the pub asking a young bar maiden to keep him informed of what passers through were saying.

Dark clouds returned with the changing of the seasons. Spring showers rained down heavily on the angelic city secretly watching over Myrinas.

*   *   *

Far to the south, near the Seas of the Damned, in the city Thiokol, an evil voice rang through the black mountains, "The time has come my brethren. We fly to war."

Two thousand wings beat in unison, sounding like the rolling thunder of the violent storm overhead. A thousand Daedra flew swiftly and undetected, above the night's storm, north toward the city of Ojai. They hovered over the great city of the Angels waiting for the signal from their fearless leader. The storm grew more violently and with a single nod, Kaelthith signaled the start of the invasion.

With each crash of lightning, Daedra fell on the sleeping city in droves of a hundred until only Kaelthith remained.

He burst through the clouds as the next bolt of

lightning reached for the ground. Screams rang throughout the city as the great dark prince broke the ceiling of the king's bed chamber. The king woke, feeling the clawed feet of the large Daedra tear into his flesh. His body burned from the venom working into his blood. The queen's scream blocked out the screams of those Angels being killed in by the onslaught outside. Hatred and vengeance burned in the eyes of Kaelthith. The Angelic king's head was forced to the side to look at his wife. Kaelthith used his free hand and stabbed two of his long, clawed fingers into the throat of the queen. Her screaming came to a sudden end, and the screams outside began to grow fainter as the Angels were cut down by the ruthless Daedra.

"Your people are all nearly dead, Baidel. Your reign as king has come to an end, and your bloodline is diminished," each word emitted from the Daedra's mouth was like the hiss of a snake. He drew back his hand and struck down as the door to the bed chamber burst open. Splinters of wood flew through the air. Aris stood in the doorway dripping from the rain and holding the sword of his father. The black blood of the Daedra covered the shimmering blade. In the darkness, the power of the sword seemed to gleam in Aris's eyes. Lines of anger covered the young prince's face. He breathed heavily as he looked up defiantly at Kaelthith.

Baidel's expression changed from a look of pain and horror to one of pity and shame at the sight of his angered son. "No!" This last word escaped the king's throat before he lay dead beneath Kaelthith's massive form. Lines of disappointment were frozen on Baidel's face.

Both of the seasoned warriors stared into each other's eyes, neither wanting to make the first move. Time itself seemed to slow to a crawl as they sized up their opponent. The drops of rain pounded heavily like boulders onto the ground. Aris tightened the grip he had on the sword of his father. Kaelthith let out a low growl. His tail draped over Baidel's body and off the bed, the tip lightly brushing over the cold stone floor, the spikes making a sharp scraping noise.

Both took flight through the open hole in the ceiling. Aris swung the sword violently at Kaelthith, while the Daedra avoided every attempted blow. Kaelthith toyed with the Angel, mocking him each time the sword missed his flesh. Finally Aris succeeded in making contact. The spiked tip of Kaelthith's tail fell and Aris caught it in his empty hand. Angered by this misfortune, Kaelthith made a sudden dive for Aris. He grabbed hold of the prince's neck with both hands and threw him towards the ground.

The streets of Myrinas were muddy, and large puddles formed throughout the square. The rain caused the heavy darkness of the late night to seem even more impenetrable. From towers over head, Half-Elf scouts watched down over the quiet, empty streets and the deserted lands in front of the city. Aris landed hard in the town square, barely able to keep his balance. Doors all around the square flew open at the sound of the crash, and spectators poured into the streets. Only a dark outline of Aris could be seen by the onlookers.

He was weary from the battle causing him to stagger. He dropped the dragonish tail and touched his hand to his side. He moved his hand, revealing a cut in his tunic from which drops of silvery blood fell freely. A bite from the Daedra had left him mortally wounded. Trying to ignore the pain, he looked up into the sky. A bolt of lightning flashed, completely revealing Aris to the townspeople. They gasped at the sight of his wings, which they had mistaken as a cloak. Lightning flashed in the sky once more. The sword in Aris's right hand was stained with black blood that dripped from the blade. Steam rose from the blood. Ignoring all those staring and pointing at him, Aris prepared to once again take flight into the storm.

Just as his feet had left the ground he was forced back down by Kaelthith. The scaly black skin of this new creature shined in the light from the surrounding buildings making Kaelthith look more sinister. His tail was wrapped partly around his body; the end missing. Sharp claws protruded out of his feet and he dug them into the skin of Aris's shoulders, trying to keep him from standing. His eyes burned red. All his attempts to keep Aris down were failing. Kaelthith was thrown off of Aris and landed on his hands and feet, sliding in the mud, skidding to a stop against a building. When Aris tried to strike, the Daedra spun around and struck with his tail, knocking the wounded Angel to the ground. Kaelthith leapt at Aris, but at the same moment, the prince blocked him with his wings and threw Kaelthith away from him. The creature half leapt, half flew away from the winged man, spinning around in the air and landing on the ground, poised and ready to strike. The winged man pushed himself up, kneeling weakly on the ground. He stretched his enormous wings and shook off the mud that had covered them. When Aris did this, it revealed something wrapped in a strange cloth strapped to his back.

Both titans stood and stared deep into each other's eyes, as if testing the other for fatigue. Aris stood to his full height, not giving away the severe pain from the many wounds inflicted on him. Both, standing over seven feet tall, circled about, waiting for the other to make the first move.

The deep, menacing voice of Kaelthith broke the silence of the pause in the battle, sending chills up the spines of the mortals, "You shall not fly away this time, Aris." Kaelthith's mocking tone filled Aris's mind with anger. "If you do, I will kill every soul in this pathetic town. So, you can die quickly tonight, or run like a coward and die slowly with the thought of their blood on your hands."

Aris's voice sent a wave of peace and calm over the people, though it carried a sense of sternness and anger, "You will not harm these people. Not tonight; not ever. I will stay and finish this Kaelthith, even in my weakened state. But unlike you, I will not destroy your race to achieve vengeance. My daughter will be able to bring back our people in time. After you are gone, my people will flourish once more, and an allegiance will be formed between the Angels and Daedra. Peace will reign once you are gone, Kaelthith. Without your influence, your race will not hold to the evil ways have you brought upon them."

With these words the battle exploded back to

life. Kaelthith leapt at Aris with such force and speed it knocked him back. Aris shifted his weight forward, and slid backwards in the mud on his hands and feet. His wings remained unmoved, held tightly in place over the bundle on his back. He pushed himself up and slashed at Kaelthith, cutting the creature's arm deeply with the tip of the king's blade. Kaelthith let out a shriek of pain. The Daedra leapt into the air, attempting to land on the Angel's broad shoulders once more. Aris bent down and grabbed the discarded tail then swung the tip, hitting the Daedric prince in the face and knocking him onto his back. Before Kaelthith could stand, Aris stepped on his chest, pinning the creature to the ground. Aris put his sword up to Kaelthith's throat.

Anger glowed like fire deep in the eyes of the mighty Angel, "I could kill you now, without a second thought."

The Daedra closed his eyes, anticipating the fall of the blade that would end his mortal life.

Aris lowered his voice and peered deep in Kaelthith's eyes seeing the fear therein, "I, however, am better than you. I will show you compassion and let you live. Leave these people, and never return. If you do not, I swear on the souls of my people, my wrath will fall hard upon you and your entire race."

Aris stabbed Kaelthith in the shoulder to discourage him from attacking again and let him up. Kaelthith, holding his wound, stood and turned to leave.

"Wait," Aris said. The Daedra stopped and turned around. Aris threw the tail at Kaelthith's feet. "Don't forget what I've told you." Kaelthith picked up the tail and fled into the rainy dark of night.

Aris watched for a moment to be sure Kaelthith would not try to attack again. He was weakened and severely injured from the battle. In an instant the mighty Angel collapsed face first into the mud. Many men ran to his aid and one of the barmaids retrieved the tightly bound bundle from his back. When she examined the bundle more closely, she found that it was baby, sound asleep. What appeared to be white silky cloth was not cloth at all, but Angel feathers. She carried the baby into the inn, following the men carrying Aris. Tables were pushed together, and sheets placed on them to act as a bed for the Angelic protector. Two Half-Elf nurses scurried over with ointments and bandages to care for Aris. When they reached his side and tried to mend his wounds he stopped them.

"It is too late to save me," he said, "My time in this life has come to an end." Even in his weakened state Aris spoke with power and dignity. The nurses backed away slowly, bowing their heads. The townspeople stood back and listened intently to the Angel.

"Liza," The barmaid holding the child stood and walked over to Aris. "My love," Aris spoke softly to Liza as she held his hand and wept. "Take care of our daughter. Raise Akarah up as a human. The time will come for her to learn her origin of her own accord." Aris brushed his free hand over Akarah's cheek and looked back up at Liza, "Goodbye, my love."

A single tear leaked from the Angel's eye. His hand loosed from Liza's, and his body went still. Liza laid her head on Aris' lifeless body and wept into his chest. The town was silent in respect to the winged man that had so willfully given his life to save them.

Several of the town's guards picked up Aris on their shoulders and began walking his body to be buried at the grave yard. A small boy watched from a distance. Everything but the boy suddenly froze still. He looked around in panic. The Angel was no longer being carried, but stood before the boy. Every where the boy turned to run, the Angel seemed to appear.

Aris looked down on the young boy, "The time has come to find my heir."

Tanas, prophet of Myrinas, woke abruptly covered in a cold sweat. He panted heavily. The message was clear; he had to find Aris's grandson.

*   *   *

Jason woke up confused and dizzy from the strange dreams of the night before. Myriad? A prophet? A lost Oracle? All of them searching for a single hero. All of them were searching for him!

2

Reunion

"Jason."

The barely audible whisper danced on a breeze through the open hallway window, dying as it reached the closed bedroom door.

"Jason."

The sleeping teenage boy barely stirred as the second whisper died at the foot of his bed.

"Jason."

The whisper bounced wildly through the air until finally entering the ears of the sleeping blond haired boy and landing in his dreams.

"Come on, Jason." Kristine's hair danced wildly in the mild wind, "I found it this time, I'm sure of it!"

Jason ran as fast as his legs would let him, but he could never seem to keep up with her. He was only ten and she was twelve so her legs were longer making her able to run faster.

"Wait up," he wheezed, stopping for a moment to catch his breath before taking off at a full sprint. He pumped his arms harder hoping that it would make him go quicker. He stopped, panting, in the entrance of the largest of the Keash caves just as it started to rain.

"Are you ever going to come?" he heard Kristine's voice echo from out of sight. Jason stepped into the cave using the wall as a guide while his eyes adjusted to the dark. A dim light could be seen from up ahead created from the flashlight Kristine brought with her. The light grew brighter the closer Jason got to the source.

In awed amazement, Kristine said, "Oh my gosh, you have got to see this Jason!"

"Where are you?" Jason asked.

A beam of light exploded out of a tunnel Jason hadn't noticed before. It was barely big enough for a full grown man to crawl through, but for children it would be easy. "Through here," Kristine answered.

Jason got on his hands and knees and peered through the tunnel at Kristine. He started crawling through when he heard Kristine gasp.

"What's wrong?"

"I lost my necklace," she said, "See if you can find

it."

Jason backed out of the tunnel feeling along the floor looking for the pendant his best friend always wore. Once he was completely out of the tunnel he turned around and spotted it on the ground right in front of it. He reached down and picked it up and yelled out excitedly, "Got it."

Then everything went black.

Panicking, he turned around and felt his way along the ground where the tunnel was but when he got there, it was gone. The tunnel had been replaced with solid rock. He tried pushing on the rock with no luck. Next, he began digging at the floor. After only a couple of inches he reached the stone beneath the dirt. Tears of frustration began running down the boy's cheeks.

"Kristine," he called out through the sobs. No answer came. Jason began to feel carefully along the rock wall hoping to find a switch to open the secret tunnel.

"Abracadabra."

"Open Sesame."

Nothing Jason could think of to open the passageway was working. Suddenly, the idea struck him that maybe she wrote down the answer in her diary. He began feeling his way blindly toward the entrance until there was enough light for him to see clearly. He stood and started walking quicker and quicker. Once he was out of the tunnel, he was moving at a run.

The rain pelted him in the face and caused him to slip once he reached the steep hill. He slipped and fell, sliding all the way to the bottom through the mud. He stood and started running again toward Kristine's house.

"Mister and Misses Simmons!" he called out as he entered the yard and threw open the door, "Mister and Misses Simmons!"

Once inside, Jason came to a sudden stop. The house was completely empty. It appeared as if it hadn't been lived in by anyone for years. Layers of dust and cobwebs covered everything.

Feeling more discouraged, Jason walked back home dragging his feet. He walked through the front door soaking wet and covered in mud. His mother looked up as the door closed behind him.

"What in the world?" she stood up and hurried over to her son, "Jason, what happened to you."

He cried uncontrollably and began rubbing his eyes with his fists. When he opened his eyes again, his mom was gone and he was in the middle of a fertile forest. Tall pine trees towered over him, the moon of a clear night peeking through the branches.

"Jason?" an unfamiliar woman's voice came from behind

Jason causing him to jump. He turned to find himself face to face with a beautiful dark haired girl tied up in a cage. A nearby man dressed in medieval garb sat propped against a tree and was fast asleep.

The woman whispered softer, "Jason, what are you doing here? Its too dangerous. You need to leave."

"Hey, what are you doing here?" the guard had apparently not been sleeping very deeply.

The young boy turned to run and tripped on a root.

Jason hit the floor next to the bed. Beads of sweat covered his forehead. He climbed up and sat down on the edge of the bed rubbing his neck. The covers were on the floor and the sheets were ripped off the mattress. It seemed ever since he found an old picture of the caves back in Ireland, the dreams of a girl being in trouble in some strange world became more vivid and frequent. This was the first time she had ever talked to him.

He looked over at the clock and let out a long sigh at the 4:24 glaring back at him. He fluffed his pillow before laying back down for a for more hours of sleep until he had to be up for his last day of high school.

*   *   *

Jason stared out the window of his mom's car. If he hadn't have wrecked his bike and had his driving 'privileges' taken away, he would have probably ditched and enjoyed a leisurely ride. Instead, his mom was driving him to school before she went to work.

Carolyn broke the silence, "I know we discussed this last night, I just want to make sure you understand how careful you have to be when riding on one of those machines. You could have gotten yourself killed!"

"What's the big deal, Mom? I barely even got a scratch on me! Besides, I'm sure I can fix the bike."

"That isn't the point. It *could* have been much worse." Her tone softened slightly, "It could be worse if it happens again."

Jason trailed off as his mother continued her usual banter about getting older and needing to be responsible in the real world. Truthfully, he didn't care much about getting a job and starting the 'typical' adult life. He wanted to go back to only place he had ever felt at home. He wanted to find Kristine; the mysterious girl that vanished eight years ago and it was like she never existed.

That's all in the past, he thought to himself. Jason just hoped his mother would forget all about it today. It was only fair, seeing as it was his birthday. Eighteen, and legally an adult at last! He had waited for this ever since his parents dragged him from their home in Ireland to come to Mount Angel, Oregon. The only benefit was the small-town living. No one seemed to care much that he just wanted keep to himself and finish high school in peace.

The plan had remained the same ever since he had come to Mount Angel. Jason already had his bag packed and tucked away at the back of his closet. His passport and money were buried in his nightstand drawer. He examined the letter he had written his mother one last time, feeling the regret building up inside him. It was difficult for him not to imagine her tears soaking the paper as he folded it and tucked it inside his passport. The day after graduation, he would be going back home. He would be going back to Ireland.

He stood up, stretching to his full height of six feet three inches as he looked at the reflection in the floor length mirror hanging from the back of his door. The amber eyes seemed a curiosity to him, as much as the slight point of his chin that made his face angular. He ran his fingers through the blond hair he had let grow to his shoulders. A soft hand felt the smooth skin on his face that had been an item of jealousy to every other teenager that suffered from break-outs, scars and freckles. It felt as if a stranger were staring back at him through the glass. *I don't remember mom or dad having any of this,* Jason thought.

He shrugged off this odd feeling, dressed and rushed out the door with a "good bye."

*   *   *

The day went by fairly quickly. He received the occasional wish of "Happy Birthday" from those that considered him a friend. He never let himself get too attached to anyone, seeing as he would be leaving and had no intention of returning.

Later that night, his father grilled steaks while his mother boiled corn and baked potatoes, then put the finishing touches on a cake. This was the tradition every year they had lived in Oregon. Jason felt a twinge of guilt as he sat to eat with his parents.

"Jason, we have something we both think you will really enjoy," his mother's smile seemed brightened by the setting sun.

This only caused Jason's stomach to drop with more guilt. A small black box was passed across the table to him. He opened it up to find a set of keys inside. Both his parents had wide smiles on their faces when he looked up at them.

"We got you a new bike, son," his father said.

Jason ran out to the garage to see a new Harley-Davidson VRSCDX Night Rod Special.

He hugged his parents, who followed him to the

garage, "Thank you so much!"

"There is also something we want to talk to you about before you go riding," his mother said, more serious now.

"I know, Mom," Jason sighed, "Be careful, wear a helmet, don't speed-"

"While that is important, it isn't what we want to tell you," his mother interrupted, and then turned to her husband.

Daniel put his arm around his son and led him to the living room, gesturing for him to take a seat. The couple sat together as Jason looked curiously between them. His father took a deep breath, "You're a man now, Jason. An adult. We both feel it is time we tell you we aren't your birth parents." Jason stared into his father's eyes wondering if this was the truth. Carolyn pulled a piece of folded piece of paper from her pocket and handed it to Jason. He unfolded the battered piece of paper revealing torn edges and a hastily scribble note.

Please take my son, Jason, into your home. He is in grave danger and I can no longer protect him. Please love him and raise him as your own.

The only sound in the room was from the old grandfather clock in the corner. Jason's parents watched him, waiting for a reaction.

"Is this all?" he choked.

His parents nodded in unison.

The guilt he had felt before began melting away.

"Why?!" he whispered. Then suddenly anger overcame him, "Why now? You lie to me about it my entire life, and just now decide to tell me."

"Sweetie, we just felt this would be the best time to discuss it," his mother said calmly.

"Right," Jason let out an angry laugh, "What a way to celebrate my birthday: Find out I'm adopted."

"It's not like that son," his father stood up, "We needed time, too."

Jason sunk into a chair across from his parents.

"Do you know who they are, or where they are from?"

His mother shook her head, "We don't, but we wish we did. We spent years trying to find out, and couldn't find anything. You were left on our doorstep with that note. Nothing else."

Jason took a deep breath, "I think I'm going to bed early tonight."

His parents stood and gave him a hug.

Carolyn kissed him on the cheek, "Happy birthday, Jason. We love you."

Jason nodded half-heartedly and walked up to his room, closing the door behind him. He lay in bed, barely sleeping that night; so many questions ran through his mind.

*　　*　　*

He rolled over as the numbers on his digital clock changed to three a.m. It was time to go. After last night, he decided not to wait. He would leave right away. He grabbed his bag, passport and money. He glanced over the note he had written for his parents.

Dear mom and Dad,

Although you have dismissed this time and time again, I know beyond the shadow of a doubt that Kristine really does exist. I have to look for her and intend to until I find her. I will come back home when I do.

Love,

Jason

Hurriedly, he scribbled one last thing

P.S. I forgive you both for not telling me sooner.

He dropped the note on his bed, then grabbing the keys to his new bike, crept quietly down the stairs and into the garage. He wheeled the bike to the street and fired it up. Taking one last glance at his parent's house, Jason rode off to the airport.

After the long ride, he left the bike in the parking garage, and went to buy his ticket. During the trip, he did not think of the life he left behind, only what he hoped to find in the place where he belonged.

Ireland was rainy, but Jason didn't care as he bought an old motor bike from someone near the Sligo airport. He paid cash and rode off, leaving the man shaking his head thinking the boy must be crazy.

Everything about the roads and the landscape felt right. For the first time in many years, Jason began to feel truly happy again. He found a town with an outdoors store and a small inn. After getting a room, he went to the store and bought everything he thought he might need for cave exploring. Several times while looking at items, he thought he noticed someone watching him, but when he looked again, no one was there. Finally, when he felt he had everything he needed, Jason returned to the inn and fell asleep.

Jason shot straight up. Rain was falling hard. He checked his watch that was on the bedside table. It was already past seven; he had overslept by an hour! Hurriedly, he threw on his leather jacket and rushed downstairs, checking out with a nod of thanks to the innkeeper.

He found his bike where he left it and turned it on; the engine choked reluctantly to life. Without a second glance behind him, he continued on to the Keash Caves he and Kristine had played in so many years ago. He didn't care about the foreboding he had that everything he knew was about to change forever.

An hour later he arrived at the cave, dismounted and attempted to hide the bike from the rain as best he could. He began digging out the provisions he had scraped up the night before. Rope, carabineers, a small pickax, hunting knife, Leatherman pocketknife, and two canteens filled with water, two waterproof flash lights, survival food packets, a heavy poncho, and an emergency blanket.

Having never enjoyed the inefficiency of matches, he had learned to use a flint and steel and put them in his backpack. He tightened the heavy boots he had acquired a year ago for backpacking the Rockies. After securing the pack snugly to his body, he felt his chest one last time. He let out a sigh of relief, feeling the pendant hanging close to his heart; the one thing he had left of Kristine's. He felt strongly it would help him find her.

He zipped up his jacket and walked to the bottom of the steep hill. The climb was difficult in the rain. The water made it very slippery, and he almost fell several times. Just inside the mouth of the cave, he stopped. He felt like someone, or something, had been following him, watching his every move. He turned around and looked back. It was useless; nothing could be seen in this heavy rain. A crack of lightning flashed down.

An image came to Jason's mind of an older man that had been watching him intently as he had been getting the supplies for the trip to this cave. The owner had thought nothing of Jason's purchase. It was obvious the majority of his livelihood came from spelunkers. It was the man he had seen by the travel guides and maps... He shook it off. Why would some old man want to follow him here? Even if he was being followed, no one would try to climb to these caves in this storm.

Another crack of lightning flashed, illuminating the cave before him. This one was closer; the thunder that followed made everything shake as it echoed through the cave. It almost sounded like a growl had answered from deep inside the dark corridor. Jason shuddered.

"OK Jason," he said to himself, lightly laughing, "let's not get paranoid now. You've done this a hundred times."

He stepped into the darkness and turned on one of his flashlights. None of the caves went very deep, though something about them felt special. Jason searched in and out of a few, remembering hiding in them all the time; remembering the games they would always play. He remembered all the legends and folklore that made them so fun for Kristine's and his imaginations. They had always hoped to find the secret doorway to another land.

Jason stood at the entrance of the last of the caves. This one went the deepest. He clutched the pendant in his hand and softly whispered Kristine's name. A bolt of lightning shot from the sky, hitting the top of the cave. Jason fell to the floor and looked up panting. It had just missed him. The rocks were red where it had hit. The air around him was warmer and buzzed with electricity. The opal sphere in the pendant seemed to be glowing. He righted himself and looked inside the cave, adrenaline pumping through his veins, pushing him forward.

He spent the better part of the afternoon walking through the cave, enjoying the familiar smell and the sound of the rain echoing through it. Memories of Kristine swam in his thoughts; everything was so familiar to him. The feelings of the love he felt were at the forefront of his mind. He regretted never being able to tell her, and knew it would be better once he could. He sighed loudly and decided to head deeper.

When he reached what he had known to be the end, he discovered something he had never seen before. There was a crawlspace just big enough for him to get through. He took his bag off and tied a rope to it so he could pull it through once he was on the other side.

Jason crawled through to the other side and shone his light all around. It opened into an enormous cavern he could not see the end of. He stepped to the edge of the cliff and looked down. Pulling his bag through, he found a glow stick, cracked and dropped it to the bottom. It hit, revealing sold ground below.

He secured the rope and prepared to start down. The rock was slippery and wet, causing him to take great care in his movements. The light hung on his belt, revealing the floor below. He glanced up one last time; it appeared as if the shadow of a man was standing at the top. He grabbed the light at his side and faced it up.
Nothing.

Thinking it was just a trick of his eyes, he went to hook the light back to his belt. It slipped from his hands. He tried to catch it but the sudden shift of weight had caused him to lose his footing. He was falling practically head first to the cave floor! It seemed as if he could feel the crunch even before the impact. Jason's back and shoulder hit first followed by the back of his head. He fought feebly to stay conscious but quickly slipped into darkness.

His eyes slightly opened several minutes later. Two men were standing over him, talking.

"What should we do with him, Seth?" the shorter of the two asked.

"We will take him with us. There is room in the Oracle's cage. There is something about him; something familiar. We will let the Dark Lord decide his fate."
Seth signaled to two other men, who picked Jason up and began carrying him. Again, Jason fell unconscious.

The next time he woke, his vision was still too blurry to make anything out. He could feel the ground rocking beneath him, and could hear the high pitched creek of wheels. He determined he was in some sort of cage. His hands were tightly bound and attached to a bar, preventing him from sitting properly. The air was warm and dry. It felt nothing like the moist air of Ireland. Everything was unnervingly quiet, aside from the sound of the carriage and whatever beast was pulling it.

He could make out the silhouette of someone else across from him. He could swear the person was staring at him. A name swelled up inside him. There was no explaining it, but he knew who it had to be. He tried to say her name, but for the first time tasted the gag in his mouth. His head sank.

"Yes Jason," The whisper came from a familiar female voice. Though slightly more mature, it was the still the same sweet voice he had never forgotten.

He raised his head slowly as the woman across from him came into focus. Long dark hair framed her pale face. She was adorned in what once must have been an elegant dress but was now dirty and torn. A soft smile accented by her deep green eyes. "It *is* me."
After all this time Jason was finally reunited with Kristine Simmons!

It dawned on Jason the predicament they were in as he took in his surroundings. Ominous dark clouds filled the sky in the direction the caravan was headed. Two thousand heavily armed men marched on the dusty highway, weary from a long march. Immediately surrounding the cage carrying Jason and Kristine, a dozen pike men and two dozen archers walked guardedly. Two black bulls walked ahead pulling the cage behind them. Two men rode horseback next to the bulls, ignoring the prisoners.

To the right, a young man no older than Jason; he appeared to be the same height as well. Shoulder-length black hair hung wildly from his head. He seemed to be trying to hide the ears that went up to a small point. His jaw line came down at a slight angle on each side, ending in a slightly pointed chin. A black tunic covered his torso, and he wore pants made of deer leather dyed black. A single sword hung at his belt, a bow and quiver on his back. Jason felt a slight tingle through his body at the sight of him. It was almost as if he knew this young man.

The second, riding to the left, did not appear to be human. His skin was grayish purple. Long, pointed ears stuck behind him and long dark hair in a single braid hung down his back. If Jason had to guess, he would have called this man an Elf. He seemed restless, as if awaiting some danger to make itself known.

The man looked straight ahead as he talked to the Elf, "Gaibian, we still have a long journey, especially with all we managed to take from Myrinas, I do not see why we cannot up the pace of the men. We've been in hiding for two years and it is clear the Dark Lord has regained most of his power. Why else would we be summoned so swiftly to return to Shirauk? I'm sure he wants to duplicate the weapons to arm the whole of his forces for a final assault on the human's city."

Gaibian turned his face to the young man, "Seth, you know full well we would be there if it hadn't been for your escapade through those caves. You taking on a new prisoner set us back at least three more days. I know the Dark Lord favors your opinion but I am certain you will have to fully explain your intentions for bringing this worthless human along. I would advise against you telling him you had whim."

"Sir?" a white-haired soldier approached the leaders, "General Seth, sir?"
Seth nodded his head in acknowledgement to the soldier's presence though his gaze remained forward; Gaibian searched the sky, not giving the soldier notice.
"Sir?" said the soldier nervously, "If the Dark Lord's word was to bring the Oracle straight back, won't he be angry we stopped to acquire another prisoner?"

"Are you questioning my command, Dorin?" Seth barked, putting the man in his place. Dorin opened his mouth to answer but Seth continued, "If I'm not mistaken, *captain*, I was given charge over this task, not you. Is this not correct?"

"Yes sir, I just-"

The captain couldn't finish before Seth cut in even louder, so he could better be heard in case others questioned him, "Then if I feel it important to deliver this man into the hands of the Dark Lord as well, I suggest you accept my decision, or count yourself among those old, broken asses we give to the ogres as lunch. Is this clear?"
Captain Dorin gave a nod and fell back in line.

Gaibian continued to search the sky as he spoke softly to his comrade, "You don't always have to be so harsh on these men. We may be able to turn some of them to fully join our cause. Over half of these men only joined the Dark Lord out of fear for their family and land, nothing more. Captain Dorin's family has been locked up until his service is completed. It is that obligation to his family that drives him. We both know many of these men are loyal to him."

"Relax Gaibian; I'm just having some fun." Seth brushed off his friend's remarks and began surveying the surrounding land.

The soldiers had noticed the approaching storm, and grumbled at the thought of marching through it. It seemed to be growing fiercer. It was moving swiftly toward them, but no wind could be felt. Both Gaibian and Seth were examining the storm now, trying to see what was moving it. Gaibian closed his eyes and listened deep within the clouds.

Gaibian's eyes shot open, "Something dark resides in those clouds, Seth. An enemy is driving that storm." One glance back at the Oracle gave the answer to what might be there.

"Ready your weapons, and protect the prisoners with your lives!" Seth repeated these orders as he rode up and down the lines, ensuring that all heard.

Bows were loaded, swords were drawn and eyes began searching the plains around them for signs of the attackers. Seth returned to the Gaibian's side; he already had his bow at the ready and was watching the storm for the creature, or creatures, within. The procession slowed. The battle-weary soldiers were suddenly alert, filled with adrenaline. The smell of a fierce battle seemed to hang heavily in the air.

The storm was nearly upon them. "Aim for the storm, but do not fire until you see a target!" Gaibian's voice carried out behind him.

Every bowman aimed for the sky as the army came to a complete stop.

"Captain Dorin," Seth's voice was firm, "you and the pike-men stand guard around the prisoners."
Without a second thought, Dorin gathered the pike-men into a tight circle around the barred wagon carrying Kristine and Jason. Kristine was shaking with fear. She had just gotten Jason back and he was about to be taken from her again, perhaps forever.

A long, low growl came from within the dark clouds. Two more echoed behind the first. No question remained as to where the attackers would emerge. Suddenly, a massive black creature exploded out of the clouds.

Shouts of "Dragon!" chorused from the soldiers. The beast landed hard on the ground, causing it to shake. Many of the soldiers lost their balance. The horses nearly threw their masters off. With this distraction, two other dragons flew down from the clouds, circling around low in the air above. The largest spread its massive wings and roared hungrily at the feast that stood trembling before him. Fire shot from its mouth into the air.

The snap of the bow string was inaudible over the roar of the fire. The arrow pierced the black creature's neck. Instantly, the flames stopped, and a cry of pain came out of the dragon's throat. Confidence returned with Gaibian's success in injuring the largest target.

Arrows began to fill the sky as archers attempted to bring down the two circling dragons. Some hit, most fell short, as the dragons dove down, then flew just out of reach, toying with the irksome men trying to shoot them. The largest let out another roar as a second arrow from Seth embedded itself into the beast's neck. Seth smiled arrogantly at Gaibian after seeing his arrow pierce deeper.

The dragon lowered its head to see the maggots that had hurt it. Both men dug their heels into their horses, running straight for the giant creature. Seth drew his sword and rode toward the creature's body. Gaibian loaded another arrow and took careful aim.

Timing would be everything.

The dragon roared at the oncoming rider with anger in its eyes. The tip of the arrow started to emit a cold burn. Confidence came with the power as it flowed to Gaibian's fingertips. He would not miss.

Gaibian released the bow string and an arrow sped through the air as the dragon opened its mouth, preparing to shoot fire at the oncoming riders. The arrow was completely covered in ice; snow-like flakes trailed behind. With pristine aim, Gaibian's arrow sailed into the beast's mouth.

Instantly the ice spread, closing off the dragon's airway. The creature began thrashing around, unable breathe. Trying to break the ice, it hit its head on the ground. This caused the creature to become disoriented. Finally, it just lay there, staring into Gaibian's eyes; neither elf nor beast broke the gaze. Hatred and hunger burned in the dragon's; focused concentration in Gaibian's. With one swift motion, Gaibian leapt from his horse and landed on the dragon's head. A dagger flew from his hand, striking the beasts left eye. With flawless symmetry, his spear thrust in and out of the right.

Gaibian kept moving, barely holding his balance as the beast flung its head upward in pain. The dragon now stood on its hind legs trying to roar. Cracks were heard from inside the beast's mouth and throat as the ice began melting and breaking apart. Gaibian found the dragon's weakest spot and forced the spear deep into the back of its skull. Instantly, the creature stopped and fell, causing the ground to shake and a cloud of dust to burst in the air.

As the dust settled, the dragon came into view. All fell silent.

The massive creature was no longer breathing. The other two dragons fled in fear at the sight of their fallen friend. Shouts of joy and praise broke out from the men at the victory brought on by their leader. Gaibian sat silently, examining the beast he had killed. Somehow it did not seem over. The skilled warrior felt that something was not right. Seth had slit the creature's belly, ready to remove the fine meat for the men. Several heavy thuds increased Gaibian's uneasiness. Ten metallic-looking spheres lay on the ground.

"Don't!" Gaibian yelled as Seth reached out to touch one. "They're dragon eggs. This was the carrier."

Gaibian knew all too well the dragons plan: Send in the Carrier- the male made to carry the eggs until they hatched. Bred to be the largest, it was usually the first meal of the hatchlings.

This would not have been the case. Had the dragon been allowed to breathe fire one more time, hatchlings would've come with it. Rather than making a meal of their Carrier they would've devoured every single one of these men. This, however, was the least on Gaibian's mind. He thought hard, trying to recall what else he had learned about the Carriers.

Seth saw the worry on his friend's face and asked, "What's wrong? We won without a single casualty." Gaibian's eyes grew wide as he remembered. "No," he said softly turning to Seth, "With every Carrier travels the-"

His sentence broke short as the cloud overhead exploded and balls of fire rained down from the sky, burning the land and killing many of the soldiers who were watching. The massive female dropped out of the sky, spitting fire at the dead Carrier, trying to hatch her dormant eggs. Gaibian and Seth barely got out of the way as flame engulfed where they had been standing. Without stopping, the magnificently colorful dragon flew directly at the wagon holding Jason and Kristine. The men stood frozen in awe at the beautiful, fearsome beast.

She roared as she approached. The men dropped to the ground as she grabbed the wagon. Her tail crashed down, crushing many of the fear-stricken soldiers that now lay on the ground. The bulls struggled to free themselves from their yolks when the dragon swallowed both of them whole.

"Stop her!" Gaibian's shouts came as he rode furiously toward the dragon.

The general's voice brought the archers back into action. They stood and started to fire at the fleeing monster that now carried the girl they had sworn to protect with their lives. Gaibian slipped an arrow into his bow after tying a rope securely to it. The swift horse carrying him had nearly caught the beast. After adjusting the fletching, Gaibian let the arrow loose. It soared through the air, spinning at first, and then spiraling wider and wider. The arrow circled the dragon's tail, wrapping the rope around it.

Gaibian took hold of the rope and pulled hard. As it went taught, Gaibian was wrenched from the horse and rose into the air. He began climbing the rope, and as he reached the tail he began stabbing it repeatedly with his dagger. The beast let out high wail of pain and lost hold of the wagon, which dropped and broke apart as it hit the trees below.

Jason winced as he felt existing cuts reopen and new bruises form as fell through the branches. Kristine screamed and reached out to him but they were quickly separated. As Jason hit the ground, he started rolling until his body hit hard against the trunk of a large tree. He grunted in pain feeling the bones in his hip and shoulder crunch, and his right arm being ripped out of the socket. Blood soaked the ground around him. He fell unconscious from the intense pain and loss of blood.

*　*　*

Kristine was found just before nightfall. The men that had not been severely injured or killed flooded the woods in search of her. She had cuts and bruises but for the most part, much to the surprise of everyone, she was mostly unharmed.

After being thrown from the dragon's tail, Gaibian had managed to suffer almost no injury at all; mostly, he was winded from the struggle with the dragons. At a quick command, a carrier was fashioned from the broken wagon pieces and the remaining men were ordered to carry the Oracle in rotations. Gaibian ordered that they would not stop until reaching Shirauk. Jason was left somewhere deeper in the woods.

3

An heir is found

The entire city was immediately called to assembly. Tanas stood before the multitude, announcing he must leave at once; the dream of so many years still fresh in his mind. Never, until the previous night, had the dream concluded. Always, the young prophet wondered why this dream had haunted him annually since his boyhood. Every year, Tanas would sit quietly during the celebrations pondering the dream.

He assured the people he must seek out the one who would rid them of the evils that haunted them once and for all. Tanas's prophecies had always been accepted; this, however, was met with mixed emotions. New rumors had started to surface that the Dark Lord had not been killed and was rising to power once again to finally overthrow

Myrinas and her people. Rebuilding of the city was still underway. The temple of the Oracle was only now reaching completion, and dozens of families remained without homes. It seemed that the peace of Myrinas since the Dark Lord's fall was over.

Though no time frame could be set, Tanas assured everyone he would return to them again, and all would be well. Many stepped up, offering their lives to the Prophet's journey. All were refused. None knew what dangers were lurking in the dark parts of the forest Tanas would travel to. None knew their deliverer was searching for this world as well. He did not yet know this was where he would find the one he searched for. Tanas had to guide the heir in this world. The Prophet must guide him to *her*.

Taking few provisions, Tanas left before sunrise the next day, while the city still slept, hoping to avoid anyone trying to follow.

"Leaving without saying goodbye to an old friend, Prophet?" Someone stepped into what was left of the dull moonlight from seemingly out of nowhere.

Head to toe, he was covered in dark red fur with streaks of grey. His face was very catlike, but he still had many features of a man. He wore a sleeveless dark leather jerkin and dark leather pants; both were tattered and worn. The jerkin was open, exposing his chest. A single scar started above his left eye and cut all the way down his body, disappearing at the waist of his pants. Below a wild main, a thick hooded cloak was tied around his neck and hung loosely down his back, covering his tail and brushing lightly on the ground. His three-fingered hands, and two-toed feet remained bare. Two identical scimitars were tied to his back. He was the only of his kind - a Raltiiri.

A slight smile was on the catlike face, "We both know you aren't going without me Tanas."

"Raza, you cannot come on this adventure," Tanas looked at his friend pleadingly, "It will be far too dangerous."

Raza laughed, "Tanas, as fast as Faer is, I can still easily keep up."

The prophet let out a sigh of concession, mounted the horse and turned away from Raza, "Keep your eyes sharp and your ears sharper. Dark days are upon us, and creatures never before seen in these lands may be nipping at our heals."

He whispered softly in the horse's ear. It reared before running off into the trees.

Raza ran on all fours, weaving in and out of the trees with the speed and agility of a cheetah.

It was near midday when the horse slowed its pace, finally coming to a stop in a thicket of trees. Tanas dismounted and surveyed the surroundings, satisfied with the cover it offered. The prophet pulled some jerky from his pack and tossed half to Raza. They ate in silence and drank from the cool river.

After an hour, the horse nuzzled Tanas. He mounted it again, whispered in its ear, and they were off. The sun dropped from the sky, making the already shadowed woods fall further into darkness. The Raltiiri made several quick glances toward the human, whose gaze remained fixedly forward. Raza had never seen his friend look so fierce and determined in the many years they had known one another.

Near the middle of the night, the horse came to a stop. Both horse and Raltiiri were breathing heavily. Slightly hidden by boulders and fallen trees, they spotted a cave that would keep them hidden for the night. Tanas removed the horse's saddle and it walked off into the darkness. Both men stepped into the cave. Raza's eyes pierced the darkness as he searched the prophet's face.

"Tanas, what is happening?" Raza's voice shattered the silence, "You have not spoken a word the entire day."

Tanas's eyes watched the ground, "The Dark Lord is gathering an army, meaning he has nearly regained his power. We still do not know who he is or where he came from, and that makes him even more dangerous."

"But, wha-," Tanas put up a hand to stop Raza.

"He has spread his evil poison across the lands; destroyed most of Myrinas. The Ogres, who before served only their lust for blood, now call him master. He has taken the Oracle. His forces seem to be without number, and still none have seen his face. Not even his closest followers know his true name, which means he could be anywhere. I feel I know who can find the answer, if he does not already know; Jerech, king of the Elves. But we must first find his son."

"He has a son?!"

"The shock, my friend, should not be in Jerech's

having a son," Tanas let out a small laugh, "But in whom his mother is." Raza stared transfixed; the air grew warm. Tanas smiled, "The boy's mother is Aka-"

He could not finish. Flames exploded into the cave, narrowly missing the two travelers. Pounding echoes filled the cave, and rock started to break away from ceiling. Tanas and Raza ran out through the opening, covering their heads.

Outside, a large multi-colored dragon was stomping the top of the cave. She stopped as she noticed the human and Raltiiri emerge. A ball of fire exploded out of the dragon's mouth, aimed directly at the Prophet. Tanas jumped out of the way and threw his now burning cloak aside. Raza was already jumping through the trees toward the creature.

"Stop!" a woman's voice commanded.

She dropped from above where Raza froze, as if from nowhere. A white silky cloak billowed behind her, a large broad sword held in her hand. Battle-worn plate armor covered her body. Only her head, neck and hands remained completely exposed. Her long blonde hair hung loosely past her shoulders. She turned to Tanas, who stood frozen with shock at her sudden appearance. Her breathtaking beauty left no question as to who she was.

"Get out of here, Prophet," she commanded.

"But how did-?" Tanas started before she broke him off.

"Run now and don't look back." -Urgent pleading entered the woman's voice- "Tanas, you must find my son. You must find Jason."

Without another moment of hesitation, Tanas turned and ran from the scene. Raza followed behind.

The further they traveled, the less they could hear the crashing and roars from the dragon. Through the dark night they traveled deeper into the woods. After several hours, dim lights could be seen ahead of them. Though exhaustion threatened to overpower them at any moment, Tanas and Raza forged on cautiously. The Raltiiri kept his hands on the hilts of his weapons; his ears perked at every snap of a twig or rustle of leaves.

Somewhere in the distance, a low creaking could be heard as a door opened and closed. Footsteps were heard, moving swiftly away from them. Raza slowly unsheathed his swords and held them at the ready.

Both men felt sharp jabs in their backs as a low, gruff voice came from behind, "I suggest you drop your swords, demon, before our crossbows *accidentally* fire."

"Dorian?" Raza asked, his grip tightening on the swords.

"Raza!?" the hostile voice turned pleasant.

The Raltiiri turned and faced his dwarfish friend, Dorian Hamber.

"They are allies, my brothers," Dorian called out.

Thirty dwarfs with crossbows in hand and axes strapped to their backs emerged from various hiding places.

Dorian looked up at Tanas pensively, "It is not mere chance that has brought you here tonight, is it?"

"No prince. I seek a human of great worth to us all; one that will bring an end to these dark days."

The prophet held the dwarf prince's gaze. Dorian raised a hand and the lights in the distance diminished.

The prince led them off to the left of where the lights had been. The whole thing had been a ruse to throw off enemies; something they practiced that had kept them safe and hidden for many years. They wove in and out of the large trees, and backtracked several times. Tanas had lost his bearings, and felt that anyone who did not know these woods, as the dwarf seemed to, would surely do the same.

The prophet was unsure of how far they had traveled before they reached some of the largest trees in the forest. They towered high above the others in the forest, and were formed in a circle around a large pond. The pond was fed from a stream flowing in; no water ran out. Dorian led them to one of the trees and looked around, receiving nods from the other dwarfs standing between the trees. He tapped lightly several times in a rhythmic pattern. The seamless trunk opened, revealing a set of stairs leading down.

They walked down the stairs that plunged deep into the earth. Torches revealed smooth stone walls. Soon it expanded into an enormous cave, where walkways broke off into several chambers. Raza and Tanas both gazed in awe at the sight. Above them, water flowed slowly downward to a deep pool beneath. This explained why the pond above did not drain out. Much of the caves remained in darkness, aside from the lit torches, which offered just enough light so no one would take a fatal step.

"The time for tours and history will come later, my friends," Dorian said to the Prophet and Raltiiri, who had slowed pace. "First, Prophet, you must tell me why I've got humans falling from the sky in my forest."

Tanas was taken aback by the spite in the prince's voice, "I am sorry, I don't believe I understand."

Dorian stopped and turned to face Tanas, "Hindling has had peace and quiet for some time. A few days ago a caravan of humans and an Elf passed by the woods, carrying prisoners from your wars!"

Dorian continued to explain about the Dragons attacking, a girl the soldiers adamantly searched for, and a young man they left behind. "All of them *human*, Tanas." The gruffness in the dwarf's voice no lighter, "We waited until dark before retrieving the boy. He is badly injured and won't speak more than a single name. We cannot make anything of it. It seems, however, that bringing him here has only brought trouble. The dragon that attacked you last night has been searching for him, and now because you decided to hide where you did, one of the entrances has been burned and caved in. It was one of our prime hunting areas, and will take months to rebuild!"

Tanas waited for Dorian to finish, his heart beat slightly quickening in excitement.

"What is the name this human speaks?" the prophet kept his voice calm and respectful.

"Kristine," answered the prince.

Tanas's excitement was harder to mask, "Could you take me to him? There is a chance he can provide answers to this whole mess."

Dorian considered it a moment, then led them down a series of passageways. It felt as if they were going deeper down. Raza glanced questioningly at the prophet, who was smiling widely. They entered a chamber that was used for medical care. Bandages, herbs and medicines sat on shelves neatly cut into the rock. Several beds were spaced along the walls. Only one held a body; a young man heavily bandaged. Four beds had been pushed together to hold him. A nurse stood and walked from the chamber, seeing Dorian and his guests arrive.

"Dorian, what else can you tell me of this human's arrival?" Tanas asked in a whisper.

"We heard some of the soldiers talking as they searched for the girl," he answered reluctantly, "They said he was found in a cave none of them had been to, and they were instructed by their general to bring him and his strange bag of items. Someone told them it was a waste of time to search for him. He commanded these men, yet strangely was not human. He was Elvish."

Tanas's eyes narrowed, and a frown formed on his face, "Do you recall any names being mentioned?"

"I believe they called the Elf Gaibian," Dorian said, "but what does that mean to you? What do you know of him?"

Tanas looked at the young man lying in the bed, "Kristine is the birth name of the Oracle. To everyone else she is known as Saedin. It is the title given to all Oracles since the beginning of time; a name they will be known by when they shed themselves of the name given at birth for the remainder of their days. The men are followers of the Dark Lord. They are some of his best warriors. Gaibian is, perhaps, his most revered general." The young man stirred slightly, "Is he heavily sedated?" Tanas asked.

"Only enough to keep him calm," the prince answered "We don't want to waste our supplies, if we can help it, but he starts to panic when he sees us. Acts like he's never seen a dwarf before."

"That is because never has," the Prophet whispered softly, so only Raza heard.

The nurse reappeared carrying a tray with hot stew and fresh bread for each of them.

"Shall I wake him, my Lord?" she asked Dorian politely.

"Yes," he answered, "Perhaps the Prophet can find out who he is."

The nurse approached the bed and woke the young man. He looked around the room with panic in his eyes, though his breathing remained steady. His gaze landed on Tanas as the prophet approached the bed. A rush of calm swept over the young man.

"What is your name?" Tanas asked as he seated himself in a chair next to the bed.

"My name is Jason England," he answered, "Where am I?"

4

The Legend of Akarah

All but Raza's eyes were fixed on the Prophet. Tanas's smile revealed he knew something about the boy. Jason looked around the room at everyone standing around him. His eyes stopped on the Raltiiri, who was looking intently at him. Raza felt something was very familiar about the young man.

"You are in Hindling." Jason's head turned at the sound of the prophet's voice, "It is a Dwarven settlement located underneath the Black Forest on the planet Myriad. I am Tanas, the prophet of Myrinas."

Jason sat up slowly burying his face in his hands trying to process Tanas's words.

"Where's Kristine?" the muffled sound broke

through his hands.

"She was taken off by the Dark Lord's army." Jason's head shot up at the news "The name's Dorian Hamber."

"So you're a dwarf?" Jason asked.

Dorian nodded.

Jason turned his head, "You're a prophet, and I'm not on Earth?"

Tanas nodded.

"And what's with the cat guy?" Jason pointed at Raza who folded his arms.

"I am a Raltiiri, and my name is Raza," he said, trying to mask the offense in his voice.

"Sorry," Jason closed his eyes and rubbed his forehead. "What does this 'Dark Lord' want with Kristine?"

"She's an Oracle. The Dark Lord wants to take her power to add to his own. We have been trying to retrieve her since she was taken away," the Prophet's eyes did not leave the young man.

"I have to find her."

"This is far too dangerous for you human," Dorian said, a little softer than his usual tone.

Jason turned toward the dwarf, "She needs my help. I have to find her!" He stood up, but overcome with dizziness, collapsed back down onto the bed.

The Prophet raised his hand to keep Dorian from retorting then turned his attention back to Jason, "Yes, you do need to find her. But before you do you need to understand everything going on."

"Fine," Jason conceded, "If you're a prophet, can you tell me what my dreams mean?"

Tanas listened while Jason told each of his dreams to Tanas. The Prophet was unsurprised by each of the dreams of Kristine's cries for help. It was the last that caught Tanas off guard.

Jason told of a large man he described as an angel fighting a "lizard-man" in a storm. He told of the lizard fleeing, the angel dying, and about the baby he had been carrying, whom he left with a woman he seemed to know. Every detail was exactly the same as Tanas's dream, except the words the angel said.

"He told me I needed to find the girl that is calling for me," Jason finished.

"The baby," Tanas looked intently at Jason, "is your mother, Akarah."

Several gasps were heard behind them.

The prophet ignored this, "The Angel is her father, Aris, and the woman is her mother, Liza."

"Wow," Jason breathed, "That is quite a tall tale. You're telling me my mom is an Angel? How am I supposed to believe all of this?"

"Open your mind, and I will show you who your mother is."

Tanas stood in front of Jason and placed his hands on his head.

Jason reluctantly did his best to relax and do exactly as he was instructed. The Prophet's voice seemed to resonate through his body, and a vision played in his mind.

*   *   *

Several years passed by as Akarah grew into a

young woman. She was never told of her father's great sacrifice to protect her. Akarah never even knew who, or what, her father was. It was kept a secret, deep in the archives to be absolutely sure she was safe. Liza wanted to protect her from the Daedra and prevent her from getting hurt. Akarah, however, had a spirit much like her father's. She wished to protect the people. Driven by her nature, and the call of the blade left by her father, she began to train with the soldiers. She gained much skill and power through the aid of her broad sword.

Akarah reached the age of eighteen and wanted nothing more than to discover who she was. This worried Liza. She feared her daughter would discover how her father was killed and seek vengeance on Kaelthith. Liza wished her daughter luck with heaviness in her heart, knowing full well there was no way to stop her headstrong ways. Akarah packed very little. She needed only her bow, sword, and great wisdom to survive. She climbed onto the great white mare, Faer, and left, seemingly flying through the morning mists. Liza held her shawl tightly around her and pleaded in her heart for her daughter's safety.

It was only mid-morning when Akarah reached the woods. She dismounted and bid the white beauty, which had carried her so many miles, farewell, saying she would call when she was needed once more. Akarah watched as Faer ran to dwell in the wild. Her composure showed great power and strength, but inside she felt only fear.

Akarah had never been outside the city on her own. She was always within the comfort and safety of city walls, or among city garrisons. Myrinas had become a safe haven to which no evil creatures could enter. Now she was alone, in a region she had never been: The Black Forest. Many had tried to explore these ancient woods, but none had returned.

Cautiously, Akarah entered the woods. A path lay ahead, covered in foliage and barely noticeable. Very little light shone through the trees above. The further in she went, the taller the trees got and the less the light made it through. Instinctively, he pulled out her sword and readied herself in case of an attack. She held her blade low at her side feigning inexperience. The light was completely gone now. She stood in the darkness, not knowing what was around her, and unable to see if anything was coming at her.

Something brushed past her face very quickly.

Akarah stood, petrified, for several seconds, in the hope that whatever had touched her was gone. She closed her eyes, put her head down, and took a deep breath. When she raised her head again and opened her eyes, there were two distinct orbs glowing directly in front of her. She gazed deeper, only to realize it was more than just a trick of light; it was a pair of eyes.

They began moving around her. Whatever it was, it was examining her. Akarah's breathing became heavy. Soon she was panicking, and her heartbeat quickened. The eyes continued to circle around her, gazing deeper upon her. It knew she was afraid.

She stabbed towards the eyes, but it was no use. She wasn't quick enough, so the eyes darted away from her and vanished. The panic became unbearable for Akarah. Cold sweat covered her palms. Wildly, she slashed her sword through the air in every direction. She became dizzy and light-headed, and the sword fell from her hand. Before she could catch herself, she fell to the ground, unconscious.

Much time had passed when Akarah finally awoke. She was inside what appeared to be a prison. It was night out, and the full-moon shone through a barred window high above. Akarah tried to stand, but only fell back to the earth. She was barely able to move any part of her, other than her head. She looked around and found a puddle of water in the far corner.

Using what strength she had, Akarah made her way to the water by scooting her body slowly across the stone floor. When she reached the puddle, she cautiously took a sip. The water tasted clean, so she drank more greedily. When the water had settled Akarah looked into the pool at her reflection. Her face was covered in blood, and she was still bleeding from a cut below her eye.

Akarah did the best she could to wash her face without the use of her limbs. She rolled over onto her back and took a deep breath. A sharp pain shot throughout her entire body, causing her to scream out. The pain seemed to never end. Once the pain finally began to subside, she heard someone laugh from the other corner of the cell.

When she looked over, she saw not a man, but some strange creature. It stepped into the light of the moon. It was an extremely large, lizard-like man. Claws protruded from its hands and feet. Its tail was nearly as long as the creature was tall. Frightened, Akarah tried to scoot into the corner away from it, but the pain had caused her body to freeze up. She was completely paralyzed.

Her state seemed all the more amusing to the creature. She tried to move again, but this only caused her more pain.

"You know," said the creature," Kaelthith says this may very well be the pain your father felt before he died."

"What are you talking about?" she winced.

"The blood of our races never did mix well. They always seem to combat one another."

The creature was now kneeling directly above Akarah.

"I-I-I don't understand," she stammered, now crying from the pain.

"Do you not know, child?" There was a pleasant, yet discomforting tone in its voice, "Kaelthith killed your father when you were just a baby. Your father fought bravely enough, but died in the end, just to spare your life."

The creature began running his claws on Akarah's face. She fought through the pain and grabbed the creature's arm. This surprised it and it threw Akarah against the far wall. Akarah grunted as she hit the ground.

"Do not hurt her again Thaelin or you will know what it feels like to drink an Angel's blood," a hideously menacing voice came from the door.

The vaguely familiar voice sent icy tingles shooting through Akarah's body. Carefully, she raised her head to look at the larger creature entering the cell.

Flashes of a great battle between a winged-man with flowing white hair and this lizard-man flashed through Akarah's mind. The horrifying face froze in her mind. She began hearing cries for help. Men, women, children, the screams seemed to echo endlessly.

Akarah was unable to hide her intense terror. Both creatures let out unremorseful laughs. Akarah shivered, and more pain rippled through her body. The larger creature was missing part of its tail.

"Sit her up!" barked the voice of the larger creature.

"Yes, master Kaelthith." The smaller creature moved immediately upon order and sat Akarah upright on a stone bench cut into the wall.

"Leave us," Kaelthith ordered, "And bring a vile of her father's blood."

The smaller creature hesitated, looking up at the larger. Kaelthith picked up the smaller creature to meet his glowing eyes, "Do it at once, Thaelin or you will enjoy the same torture she has."

Thaelin was hurled out the door and he quickly ran off down a hallway.

Kaelthith stood in front of Akarah and looked down upon her. She gazed back at the creature, trying to mask her fear.

"You are going to kill me, aren't you?" she asked.

"Not just yet," Kaelthith laughed, "You have not suffered enough."

Again, Akarah spoke, "What did he mean about races' blood not mixing well?"

"Simple child, Daedric blood is like poison to Angels, and Angelic blood is like poison to the Daedra."

"Angels? But I am human."

"You are so naive about your past, child. You are the final descendant of the Angelic race. Your father and I fought a grueling seven-day battle before I was finally able to get enough of my blood into him. I would have killed you as well, had I known of your existence.

"When I learned he had left a child to the humans, I wanted to take you for myself. I, however, had greatly suffered and was too weak to come after you. My people also suffered too great a loss to attempt to try taking you from the humans. You can't imagine my elation when you ventured from the safety of the city alone."

"No, it is not true! My father was human He was a hunter, not a warrior; he never fought a battle in his entire life. He-He was killed by a pack of wolves while hunting."

"My patience with your ignorance is spent. Your father, Aris, was an Angel. You are an Angel. Because of your father's clever ruse, I was momentarily prevented from destroying your race, but now I have the chance. Do not worry though; I will not kill you quickly, as I did the rest of your pathetic race. You will die slowly and painfully. You will feel the same pain that I felt for so many years as my body recovered. You will first face my pathetic excuse for an older brother. I want to enjoy watching you ripped to shreds." A sinister smile stretched across the face of the Daedra.

"I can't even move. And I need my sword to fight."

"Don't you worry, child, you will be able to move soon enough. As for your sword, you did not have one when you were brought here. Thaelin will not be using a weapon anyway. Why should you?" Kaelthith walked from the room, laughing.

Thaelin reentered the cell holding a small vile in his scaly hand. Its slivery glow appeared brighter than the moon.

Thaelin put the vile to Akarah's lips, "Drink this so you can regain the use of your limbs."

Akarah drank hesitantly at first, but then found the liquid to be warm and soothing. It tasted sweet like honey. As soon as the warmth hit her stomach, all the pain she felt was gone. She drifted off to sleep as she heard the cell door closed and locked

* * *

She dreamed of a kind man who cared dearly for her. The man beckoned her to him, calling her by name. The voice faded and she was stirred from her sleep by a nearby presence.

A wet rag was on her forehead. Akarah slowly opened her eyes, hoping to see her mother's face. Once her eyes opened, she saw a hooded figure kneeling next to her. All she could see was one red, glowing eye in the midst of blackness.

A low, hoarse voice spoke from within, "Young one, your time to face my eldest son is soon at hand. Though Thaelin is older, Kaelthith commands this people. I am old and weak, but still have some sway over this race. Do not fret young angel, you will be spared the pain my wicked sons have promised you; this much I can promises you.

"Listen closely, young one, and heed my words. Thaelin will attack swiftly. He wishes to injure his prey, and then make them suffer a slow death. His heart is not as black as his younger brother's, though he fears Kaelthith. But you need not worry, young one. I sense your father's great spirit and power inside of you. If you do not embrace what you are, you will not survive my eldest son. My time in this life is nearly spent. I am old and the acts I have and will cause will turn my younger son completely against me."

The wizened Daedra removed his hood, revealing his damaged face. He was missing one eye and there were many places where scars had formed or chunks had been taken from his face. Although frightening, the face and voice were very kind and gentle. Akarah never learned why he had shown mercy on her that day.

The old Daedra got up to leave.

"Wait," Akarah stopped him, "Who are you?"

The Daedra turned back to face her and took her hand, "I am called Bahamut. I have lived long enough to see how great your people can be, though this is never how my son will view it. I have kept peace in this world as long as I can. However, peace may not be meant to live."

Again, Bahamut turned to leave, and Akarah stopped him once more, "What do you mean? And where is my sword?"

The ancient Daedra closed his eye.

"Once I am gone, Kaelthith will gain complete rule over the Daedra in my place. He wishes to take control over all of Myriad. As for your sword, "Bahamut let out a weak laugh, "It was never found. My son does not know of its great potential power. I forged it for your grandfather and I alone know its true power. The sword lies within you, young one.

"I have one more thing for you." Bahamut reached into the confines of his cloak and pulled out a ring, "This was created by your grandfather and me long ago. The jewel is made from a piece of both of our hearts and is indestructible. It holds great power that not even I have fully discovered. You will use it for greatness; my son only for evil if he discovered it."

The Daedra placed the ring in Akarah's hand and left. Two teardrop shaped gems – one the purest silver, the other darkest black - encased in a circle of metal Akarah recognized as the same metal the blade of her sword was made of. Kaelthith showed up shortly after the wizened old Daedra Bahamut had left, "It is time."

Akarah did not understand what Bahamut had meant when he said the sword lay within her, and it seemed time had run out.

He grabbed her and dragged her to a large arena. All around Daedric eyes watched her thrown into the arena. Dozens of dragons patrolled the skies. She knew there was no hope of rescue or escape. She placed the ring on her finger that she had been clutching tightly in her hand, and immediately it formed to fit perfectly. She felt confident with the ring on.

Akarah turned a complete circle searching for Bahamut but never saw him. She feared that he was already dead. A large platform overlooking the arena on the south end housed Kaelthith. His brother Thaelin stood next to him. Thaelin appeared fiercer than ever, though there was a hint of fear in his eyes. He knew if he failed his brother, it would be his final mistake.

Akarah scanned the arena grounds in hopes she would find her blade laying among the rock and sand. She knew there was no chance of surviving unarmed hand to hand combat against Thaelin. Not even a week had passed since Akarah had left Myrinas, and her life would shortly come to an end. Thaelin leapt into the pit, landing hard on the rocks. Cheering erupted throughout the crowd. Thaelin walked to the middle of the grounds and stretched his wings to their full span. The cheering continued to rise. Kaelthith raised his claw into the air and all feel silent. All that was heard was the occasional flap of wings from the dragons above. Fear once again gripped Akarah, and her heartbeat quickened.

The commanding voice of Kaelthith filled the

silence, "We have gathered to witness the end of our enemies' bloodline, once and for all. For too long we have allowed her to live, but we will end it now. Thaelin, you will slay her now, or lose your life."

The crowd roared their approval.

Thaelin spread his wings again, and flew straight at Akarah. Akarah covered her face awaiting the blow from Thaelin. There was a loud crunch, and the crowd fell silent.

Akarah opened her eyes and looked down. Thaelin's lifeless body lay crumbled at her feet, and her sword was in her hand, covered in black blood. All around the crowd grew angry. No one understood how this could have happened. She had been unarmed. Arguments arose amongst the spectators. Fighting broke out in the stands. Only Kaelthith was left watching her. Anger was in his eyes at his pitiful brother, who had failed to carry out his task.

Kaelthith knew it was up to him now. Daedra were fighting amongst each other. Wounded and lifeless bodies were being thrown into the arena. Kaelthith arose from his seat and flew at Akarah. He dove, and Akarah ducked. As she did this, a large silky feather cloak covered her body.

She stood again ready to defend herself. This time Kaelthith flew at her torso. Instinctively, she leapt into the air, soaring high above the ground. She turned around and realized she wasn't falling back down. Before Kaelthith could come at her again, an enormous shadowy, gray dragon with torn, leathery wings and one eye grabbed her, and carried her away. It turned and shot fire back at Kaelthith causing him to fall out of the sky to the ground.

The dragon soared through the clouds late into the night, and soon Akarah was sleeping. When she woke again, she was lying in a soft, feathery bed. She got out of the bed and walked through the open door and found herself on a balcony. An enormous city lay quietly before her. Cracked buildings choked with overgrowth were below her, all surrounding a fountain directly in the middle. Statues of winged men and women lined the streets to the entrance of the building she was in. Akarah guessed this had once been a palace, for it overlooked the entire city she knew had once been elegant.

A bony, clawed hand touched her shoulder, and she nearly fell from the balcony. The wizened old Daedra, Bahamut, stood behind her.

"I thought you were dead," Akarah said, her voice

filled with relief to see him.

"I soon will be," he replied, "It took too much of my power to transform into a dragon again to save your life. What is left of my power, I have given to you." – He pointed at the ring on Akarah's finger – "It will help in your journeys. It will fortify your blood and the blood of your offspring. I feel you will accomplish many great things, daughter of Aris. When you killed Thaelin and I brought you here, the binds staying my son's wrath were broken. The final war between our peoples has always been inevitable. Now that he knows you are alive, my son will hunt you ruthlessly. You are the only one living that will be able to fend off the armies of Kaelthith. When you are stronger and wish to know more of who you are, travel south across the Seas of the Damned to the Isles of the Dead."

Bahamut took Akarah's hand and she felt his life and power filling her. "Six orbs will remain here when I die. Before you go to the Isles, deliver them to Jerech in the Black Forest. The orbs will show you the way."

A tear ran down Akarah's cheek as Bahamut expelled his last breath. The wizened old Daedra that had saved her life was gone. The body turned to ashes and was carried away by the wind. As he said, six orbs remained behind. Akarah picked them up and left the great palace. She traveled back to the Black Forest where she had been attacked. There she found Jerech.

They quickly fell in love and were married.

After years of hiding from Kaelthith's army she became pregnant. Before giving birth, she traveled to Earth to keep him safe from all that took place on Myriad. She did not want her children hunted as she was. He was left on Earth, and almost none knew of his birth. She remained in hiding, silently protecting Myrinas from the evils that threatened it. The day came when she vanished completely. Few ever saw her; they only heard stories of her heroics. All believe the day will come when she will be seen again.

5

An Unexpected Return

Deep within Shirauk Mountain, the city below the Dark Lord's fortress was being torn down – along with all the villages near the mountain's base. All who refused to give up their homes willingly were killed. The scrap from the city was being used to create massive war machines. Any food and supplies were taken to the store houses. Plans were delivered into the hands of Seth, and construction of the machines began. The goal was to have the machines built within the month, and to attack Myrinas shortly thereafter.

Within a week, only skeletons of buildings remained. Large pumps ran to the river deep in the canyon, to provide an adequate supply of water. Work went on ceaselessly, both inside and out of the walls of Shirauk.

Weapons and armor were being made. Training was underway for seemingly endless recruits of Orcs who bent to the will of the Dark Lord. Never before had an army of this size been gathered for a single purpose. Nothing was to be spared in the attempt for control of Myriad and its sources of power. Every last available resource was to be used. Weapons, food, and water began piling up, and soon prisoners were crammed together to make room for the cache of supplies. When there was no more room for prisoners, they began being used as target practice for the Scythians, a race believed to be extinct. The Scythians spread terror everywhere, killing for sport and nothing more. The Dark Lord took control of them as soon as he found the last of them hiding in the caves of Shirauk.

Men worked furiously until the setting of the sun. At this time, massive drums beat to alarm the change of shifts. The men who had just finished returned to nearby tents, to the North of the machines. At the same time, men emerged from tents to the South to work through the night. Massive bonfires climbed high into the air. Mirrors were placed, reflecting light to every last inch of the grounds. Hammering, clinging of swords, and screams from the slaughtering of prisoners echoed through Shirauk.

The last of the prisoners were released into Shirauk forest. An hour passed, and the most skilled Scythians followed on horseback. Panic and horror filled the air as the thundering of twelve hooves roared in the ears of the one hundred fifty prisoners. It didn't take long before the slowest of the prisoners were overtaken by the blood thirsty warriors. Screams erupted as the elderly, sick, and disabled were killed. The remaining eighty-seven prisoners listened as the screams were cut short within seconds, and all was left silent, except for the rustling of the leaves from the light breeze coming from the East.

A cry from a young girl came from behind the group. A distraught mother searched frantically, trying to retrace their steps. The cries stopped and the woman fell to her knees weeping at her loss, and knowing she would lose her life next. A sword fell, and one last tear from the mother's eye hit the ground.

Panic grew as screaming infants were torn from their mother's arms. Distressed parents pressed on, knowing if they stopped, they too would die. All knew the time to mourn for loved ones would come, once this nightmare ended; if there was an end.

The remaining thirty-one men and twenty women

reached the center of the forest. The moon was full, and the sky had no stars. During planting and harvest season, the sky was always empty discouraging travelers from going very far. Only skilled hunters and wanderers with no set course were known to travel this time of the year. This gave them all hope, knowing the armies could never reach Myrinas without the guidance of the stars. Even the Dark Lord's power could never guide such a large army without the guidance of the stars. Too many would lose their way.

Though weary, the released prisoners pressed on. Before leaving the clearing, the men found swords, shields and spears laid about. A cold fire pit was nearby. They feared it to be a trap, but their hope was all but spent. The men armed themselves, feeling a sense of protection as they attempted to escape the forest. They were all weak and hungry, but their determination to be free outweighed everything else. Once the last of the group left the clearing into the pitch of the forest, the thundering sound of hooves surrounded them once more. Sound bounced off the trees making it impossible to tell how many there were, but there was no question as to whom rode the horses. The Scythians' lust for death had not been satiated. They had surrounded the prisoners to prevent them from fleeing the forest.

Men readied themselves to defend the women and each other. As they foraged deeper into the darkness, the thundering increased. A hooded man issued whispered instructions to follow a small stream. This was the first time anyone noticed the water next to them. The man went silently to the right with only a small sword in hand. All obeyed the stranger that had seemed to have been guiding them all this time.

Several more hours passed before three more women screamed as they were dragged in different directions by ropes wrapped around their legs. Seconds later, three men hung by their ankles up above. Some men scrambled to try to rescue the women, while the rest began climbing to cut down those hanging over head.

One of the men caught up to the woman he'd pursued. He'd been alone in following her. It was hard to follow because of the great speed at which she was being dragged, but he was determined to catch her. They had just married before being imprisoned. He reached her as she came to a stop. Her body was bruised and she was bleeding but she was still alive. The man stepped towards his wife who reached for him. His approach was cut off by a Scythian when it stepped onto his wife's outstretched hand. She still had no breath to cry out, but the pleading in her eyes told her husband of the pain she was in.

The Scythian let out a snake-like hiss that sounded much like a laugh as the man stepped to attack. The six foot man stood before the eight foot monster. As the man lunged forward, the Scythian side stepped. A trap released, whipping the man and his wife upside down. They were now suspended facing each other far enough apart that their finger-tips could barely touch.

The woman reached her husband's hand. Before he could raise his hand, his body went limp. A dart protruded from the side of his neck. A look of fear and pain was left in the man's eyes. The twang of a bowstring was heard from behind the woman. An arrow brushed close by her face followed by the ringing of metal on metal. The Scythian screeched in pain as another arrow struck where a heart should have been.

The heartless body fell to the ground and broke into a pile of dust. The woman was cut loose, fell and was caught by their guide who had run off alone.

There was warmth in his voice, "You are safe now. The others are waiting."

There was wonder in the woman's eyes as she pondered the familiarity of her rescuer's voice. He set her down on her feet then cut down the limp body of her husband. Tears erupted from her eyes as she heard him take a deep breath. The man she loved was still alive, but too weak to walk, or to even move. Their rescuer carried the man until they reached the remaining thirty men and women. He was placed on a stretcher made from a Scythian cloak for a more comfortable trip.

An hour more passed before the remaining thirty-three prisoners reached the clearing of the forest. All drank greedily from a nearby pool of untainted water. The man everyone revered as their leader tended to the man he had saved. An antidote to the poisoned dart was poured in the man's mouth. The others recounted the tail of how the leader had gone hand to hand with a Scythian and stabbed it in the chest killing it without so much as a scratch.

Though the loss of the other hundred twenty-seven prisoners hung heavily over them, all except the leader slept. He stayed awake and alert at all the sounds and movements of the night. Two hours before sunrise, the woman he had saved woke.

"I never thanked you for saving my husband and

me," her voice was still tired and weak.

The leader continued staring into the forest, "We aren't safe yet; one of them is still out there. You should rest; we will leave in an hour."

"But first," she said, "I have to know. Are you -" she choked not able to finish her sentence.

He turned to her, his face shadowed by the hood, "Don't worry about who I am. You will all know when we reach Myrinas."

Before another word could be said, the leader caught an arrow as it nearly struck his eye. Wrapped around was a scroll with strange writings on it. The sound of hooves faded away toward Shirauk as the leader read the scroll in silence.

"It's time to leave," his voice woke everyone and they left immediately without hesitation.

Questions came from all around as they forged on.

Without looking at anyone, the leader answered each question, "Scythian warriors. Heartless spawn that were once murders, rapists and bandits. An evil that kills for pleasure. They wanted to kill us to *kill*. They were commanded to kill us to make room for supplies and weapons for the Dark Lord's armies. If it wanted to kill me, it would have. It wanted me to live to deliver a message to the Prophet. The scroll is of no concern. Its contents are for the Prophet alone."

With finality he said, "We are going to Myrinas. There is much preparation for what's to come. And we have to get there before the setting of the sun. Save your breath."

All kept quiet the remainder of the journey. They reached the city as the sun was setting on the Western horizon and the full moon rose in the East. People of the city began whispering to one another at the site of their leader. The now free prisoners dispersed to their homes to reunite with their families and at long last, get a good night's rest. The gates were closed and all was still as far as the eye could see.

The following morning everyone gathered to hear how they had all survived the journey. The hooded leader stood before everyone and offered his warning of the impending invasion. Much murmur came from the gathered crowd. The people of Myrinas were growing even more frightened. The absence of the Prophet had gone on several weeks now and they wondered if they would ever see him again.

The leader put his hand up to silence the crowd, "I know you are afraid but I am here to put an end to this. I have spent much time listening to the whisperings of the guards and know what is coming."

Their spirits rose at the sound of such a commanding yet calming voice coming from beneath the hood.

"The dark days that have long been prophesied have come," slowly he removed the hood, "And I tell you there is no need to fear."

Not a sound escaped from onlookers. Before them stood a man they believed to be dead; believed to be slain by the hand of the Dark Lord. Silamond, the former prophet of Myrinas, was alive.

He ignored the awe struck faces about him, "Where is my son? Where is Tanas?"

"Sorry prophet," one of the guards stepped forward, "But I am afraid he left weeks ago and has yet to return. We don't know where he has gone."

6

Council at Midlothian

Jason's determination only increased after being shown a brief glimpse of his mother. Over the next several weeks as his health improved Jason began to train with Raza as much as he could. Though discomfort remained toward the Raltiiri, Jason's desire to be able to save the girl he loved proved stronger.

For hours the two would spar with swords and staves. Jason's tattered clothes had been discarded and he had been given clothing more fitting to Myriad that the dwarves had made up for him. He learned surprisingly fast for never having fought in his life. At the end of every day he would plea with Tanas to let him go after Kristine. Tanas always refused, saying there was still too much for him to learn.

By the end of the fourth week Jason's patience was spent, "I've had enough of this! You keep telling me I'm not ready, and that I have to be more powerful to face the Dark Lord. I'm not here to kill him! I'm not this great hero you keep talking about! I just want to get Kristine back and go home."

Tanas sighed, "The only way the Oracle can be freed is to defeat the Dark Lord, and he is far too powerful for you to face right now. He possesses terrible dark magic. To get to him you have to get through an army of thousands of dark creatures and evil men."

"I don't care," Jason shot back.

"You should care." A man emerged from the shadows neither Jason nor Tanas had noticed. His hair was long and matted. His face held scars from past battles. A long bow and quiver were on his back. Two long daggers hung at his belt. His pants were dirty and torn. His chest was bare, revealing more scars. A tattered brown cloak hung on his back. His feet were bare. What struck Jason the most was not his ragged appearance, but his skin. It was a dark, earthy purple. His long ears poked backwards out of his long hair and were nothing like a human. Though he had the look of a peasant, he held himself like a leader.

"Let me guess, you're an Elf?" Jason asked sarcastically.

The elf nodded.

"Right; and you're probably here to tell me my destiny is to be a hero and save all these people I have never even heard of," Jason stood with his arms folded.

The Elf smiled, "You make very astute observations. If you already know that, you should also know that only you direct your path. You choose what destiny lies ahead of you. However, if you want to find this girl, it would be in your best interest to hear what I have to say."

Jason sat on the ground crossed-legged, "Fine, I'll listen if it means finding Kristine." He looked up at the Elf. Something in those eyes made Jason feel a strong dislike toward him.

"I am a messenger from the Elven city Midlothian," the Elf began, "You can call me Orin. News of your arrival has reached our council. Our king seeks an audience with you. He can tell you more about who you are. He can also tell you where to find your Kristine. If you accept, we must leave immediately."

"Good. Let's go," Jason jumped up eagerly. *Finally, I will get some answers*, he thought.

As Orin promised, they packed up and left right away. Since the dwarfs had no horses to lend, not having use for them, the four traveled on foot. At the head was Orin, with the Prophet walking at his side. Several paces behind were Raza and Jason. Tanas and Orin talked animatedly to one another in a loud whisper, though Jason could not make out what they were saying.

They followed Orin into the canyon that split the forest in half. Jason fought to be as patient as he could; he had been away from home just over a month, and until this point, regretted no decision he had made so far. He walked in silence, reflecting on the mistakes he had made. If only he had taken more care back in the caves, perhaps everything would be different. Maybe Kristine would be safely by his side now, and they would be going back to Earth.

Back to Earth? Jason laughed inwardly at the thought.

This was all ridiculous. So much of it was too conveniently close to all the dreams he'd had since he was little. There was no humanly possible way this could real.

Even for a dream it was pretty crazy. This, Jason assumed, was because he had hit his head when he fell in the cave. It was decided: this was all just a wild dream. He was either still lying on the cave floor, or in a hospital bed after someone had found him. He would just go along with the dream until he woke up. Maybe the dream would help him figure something out, and when that time came he would continue searching for Kristine, and go home when he found her.

Thoughts of home brought on mixed emotions. Jason sighed as he thought of the people that had raised him. Even though they had kept the adoption from him, he felt he still owed something to them. As soon as he could he would call and apologize for leaving the way he did. A slight twinge of resentment toward his biological parents crept up his spine. He wanted to know the reason they had abandoned him. For now he would have to try and push that to the back of his mind.

He still didn't care much for the Prophet. *What choice do I have,* Jason thought, *this is probably the way to get through this stupid dream. The prophet is probably a subconscious guide.* More importantly, maybe he would be able to find Kristine in this mess. At least for the time being, Jason would continue traveling with the group.

Clouds began to close in, carried on a cold wind. In a matter of minutes they were hindered by large drops of water from the sky. The rain slowed the progress of the party as the ground became muddy. They had to take greater care with every step they took. No pathways existed to where they were going. The Elves obviously had no desire for visitors, and it was easy to keep it that way since the rain storms reformed the land often. The trust of the group lay with Orin on getting them to Midlothian safely.

The rains cleared as the trees became less dense. The last of the days light leaked through the trees as night fell. The roar of a river could be heard ahead of them. They broke through the trees. To the west, the river disappeared around a bend. To the east, it fell over a cliff. Directly in front of the party, a stone bridge stretched from the south bank to where they stood on the north bank. At each corner, towers stood as sentinels over the bridge. Directly in the center stood two more towers, twice as large as the ones on the ends. The stone was covered with moss, and vines of ivy stretched to the tops of the towers. As a whole, the structure appeared as if it had been abandoned for years, though it did not seem to have fallen into disrepair.

Orin watched as Jason marveled at the size and obvious durability of the bridge. The swift, powerful pull of the river had no effect.

"Step lightly, kid," Orin laughed as Jason slipped on the moss. He helped Jason back to his feet, "If we were ever to be invaded, this is our first line of defense. No one takes caution when crossing an abandoned bridge. Once the front lines of any army is nearly across, the archers hidden in the towers start firing. The surprise of a sudden attack will cause the army to slip on the moss as they attempt to fall back and defend themselves."

"But wouldn't it seem like an obvious trap?" Jason asked condescendingly.

"More so to us Elves than anyone," Orin replied, "Humans take too much stock in appearances. They would never allow such a vital outpost to become 'overgrown' like this. We, however, take more pride in the things that grow; even help them as much as we can, and they help us out in return."

Stepping more carefully now, Jason followed Orin across the bridge.

Immediately on reaching the opposite bank, most the discomfort Jason felt toward the Elf went away. Something about being in this place felt almost like home. He relaxed more and began talking to them all about where he had come from and all about growing up with Kristine. As he talked about traveling on Earth, it was clear Tanas did not care for the idea of airplanes, but Raza and Orin were equally entertained. They even joked about going there when all of this was over to fly in one.

Jason began to tell Orin how he had ended up on Myriad and been so close to Kristine. He came to a sudden stop as the plethora of emotions became too much. "I'm tired, is it okay we stop and rest for the night?"

Orin nodded in understanding and laid out mats on the ground. Despite the rain, the ground and air were quite warm.

"We'll leave before sunrise," Orin instructed.

Jason lay down facing away from the rest of the group and pretended to fall asleep quickly. Tears fell silently from his eyes.

"Good night boy," he heard Orin whisper behind him. Jason soon found sleep shortly after. He dreamed much like he had before coming to this place.

In the midst of black mountain fortress in the tallest tower a beautiful girl was locked away. She sat huddled on the cold stone floor, crying openly.

"Where have you taken him?" she asked through her sobs, "Please, I want to see him."

Kristine's pleading cries were ignored, if anyone had heard them. She was utterly alone. With the little strength she had left, she stood and walked to a window facing the east. Far away on the horizon the first ray of light could be seen trying to break out across the land.

With what little hope of freedom she had left, Kristine began shouting, "Jason! Jason! Jason!"

"Jason."

Someone was shaking him.

Jason shot straight up, "Kristine?!"

He looked around and saw the scar covered elvish face looking worriedly at him, "No, it's Orin. Are you all right? You've been flailing around like rabid wolf."

"Yeah, I'm fine," Jason wiped the sweat from his face.

"Good; let's go," Orin said.

The party got up and began walking again. Jason said nothing about his dream to anyone. The sun still had not risen on the horizon when they reached a large wooden gate built into a stone wall. Much like the bridge, the stone wall was covered with moss and ivy. The Elf approached and knocked hard. A small window opened and an Elven sentry poked his head out.

He looked from Orin to the others and scoffed, "Hope these are friends of yours. You know humans are not openly welcome here."

"I think they will be welcomed by the council, and it would be unwise for you to question my judgment in bringing them here."

The window closed and the gates were opened, admitting the Elf, the Raltiiri, and the two humans. The sentry glared as he watched them walk away.

Inside the wall was a much different sight than any of them expected. There were paved streets, gardens, and orchards with all types of fruits. In the distance another wall could be seen. Elves emerged from the open doors and began tending to the gardens and orchards. Jason counted only three walls. The one behind them, to the south, one to the west and one in front of them, to the North.

Orin answered the question before it was asked, "The city is built on the cliff so there is no need for an East wall. No one is foolish enough to try to bring an army up the cliff face. They would be killed before making it even half way."

As the people noticed Orin and his companions they began pointing and whispering. They glared at Jason and Tanas, and stared questioningly at Raza.

"Don't pay an attention to them;" said Orin, "Much of the hatred still burns between the humans and pure blood Elves ever since the Alliance of Races broke."

It seemed no one dared approach Orin and ask why he would bring two humans into their land. They turned east and approached the second wall. It seemed to tower higher than the first. Several archers could be seen lining both the inner and outer walls.

As they passed through the second gate, Jason's

heart began to beat faster with excitement. Suddenly the sun broke over the horizon, flooding the entire city with light. Beautiful houses could be seen lining the streets. Children started running out of doors excitedly. More men and women emerged from the houses. Each of the Elves shared a similar complexion as Orin, though none shared the same scars.

The clothing was simple and yet, as with everything about the Elves, was beautiful. Work began at the blacksmith's and the stables. No merchants seemed to be present anywhere.

Again, Orin answered the questions on the minds of his companions, "The success of our city is not measured in great treasures but in its people. Everyone works together equally. They are given sufficient for their needs, and all take turns working the gardens and orchards, or caring for the livestock and flocks, or the horses in the stables. Everyone remains happy and peaceful."

The beauty of the city soon fell to the back of everyone's minds. Before them stood an elegant castle. The wood and stone works were all carved with intricate designs. Above the entrance to the castle, a crest had been cut into the stone. Inside, a blue carpet ran down the middle of the marble hall ways. Orin led the group into the large council room.

Enormous tapestries hung on the wall bearing the crests of past kings. Six small, glowing spheres lay evenly spaced in the center of a large round table in the center of the room. At the head of the room, atop several stone steps, were two large thrones. Two smaller thrones stood on each side. Hanging over the thrones was a tapestry with the same crest that was carved above the castle entrance. As with the rest of the castle, shapes and symbols were carved into the walls and ceiling. Delicately crafted statues of the wives that ruled with the kings stood underneath the tapestries. A man in a black hooded cloak stood at one of the statues.

Orin walked over and placed his hand on the man's shoulder. They spoke quietly to each other for a moment. The hooded man turned and began walking toward the other two men. Anger welled up inside Tanas as the hood was removed, revealing the Elf's familiar face. Jason knew he recognized the him, though struggled to recall from where.

"What are you doing here?!" the prophet yelled, "You should be killed for what you have done!"

"Tanas," the Elf said calmly, "You do not understand the circumstances. I am here to bring report of the Dark Lord's activities."

"You are here to act as a *spy* for him!" Tanas walked forcefully toward him. Orin came between them, facing Tanas.

"Prophet," Orin said, "I called him here. He has been spying for us and has done so quite well. Because of him we may be able to discover the true identity of the Dark Lord."

"Gaibian is a traitor to all that is good, and should be killed," the Prophet shot back.

The set Jason off. He drew his sword and ran at Gaibian. "Where did you take her?" he yelled. Before he knew what had happened, Jason found himself on the ground with the tip of Gaibian's dagger against his throat.

"You're a fool of a human," Gaibian said.

A hand grabbed the back of Gaibian's cloak and he was thrown backwards.

Orin stood over Jason protectively, "You will not

threaten my son!" The shock at this revelation vibrated through the room. Jason took the outstretched hand offered by the Elf that had called himself Orin.

"You? But you said…," Jason stuttered over his words.

"Yes, Jason, I am your father. I am Jerech, king to the Elves of Midlothian," he smiled warmly at Jason. Jason looked more closely at Jerech for the first time. He noticed they shared the same angular face. Though they were not long like the rest Elves, it occurred to Jason for the first time that his ears were pointed. Jerech's gaze was fixed on his son and the amber pigment in his eyes seemed to glow.

Questions would have to wait. Just then several servants entered carrying plates of food, goblets, and pitchers of wine. They placed them at each of the seats at the table. As they exited, Jerech's council of twelve filed in and filled the seats: six women and six men. Jerech gestured for Jason and Tanas to sit on either side of him. Two extra chairs were brought in for Gaibian to sit next to Jason, and Raza next to Tanas. Jerech was the last to take a seat. Everyone ate in silence.

After the meal, the same servants entered and

cleared the table. The doors were then shut, and none were allowed in or out. There were no windows in the room, nor any torches lit. The only light came from the six orbs in the center of table. Each one glowed just enough that they created a ring of light barely larger than the table. The rest of the room remained in total darkness. Whisperings floated around the table. Inquiries as to who the strangers were that filled the normally vacant seats. Jerech stood, and the council silenced at once as he began to speak:

"My most trusted and loyal friends, I thank you for coming at such short a notice. I know it is out of our nature to call council so soon, but I assure you it is necessary at this time. The enemy is spreading its plague. I know many of you question my reasoning for bringing humans to our land. You all know of the man to my left. He is the son of Silamond, the prophet. His name is Tanas, and he, also, is a prophet of Myrinas"

Many nodded in understanding, though still reluctant to accept his presence.

"The other," He gestured to his right, "is a stranger not only to our people, but to all of Myriad. This young man is my son." Gasps came from each council member. "I know you heard rumor he died at birth, but this was only to keep him safe. He was raised on Earth as a human. He has trained the past month with the Raltiiri, Raza, and will continue to train with us. He will learn to fight as we do, for his is a destiny greater than any of us can truly understand.

"Now for the other reason I have called you here. The war is spreading as the enemy grows stronger. We had sworn we would never again aid the humans when they banished us from their lands. Our half-human brethren remained with them in Myrinas, at my request. I know of your objections to this, but my decision was made in love for the people. The protection of Myrinas is important to more than just the humans. The city holds a greater key to all of our survival more than any of us can fully comprehend. The time is coming close for the alliance of old to be reunited."

Shouts of objection came from all around the table.

"Please," Jerech said, "bear with me." The room again fell silent, "In a very short time, Myrinas will be overrun by the army of the Dark Lord. Even as we speak, his forces move from Shirauk. They are led by a throng of Scythian warriors. Most of his captains were picked from among them. We've all seen the devastation Scythians cause. They are one of the greatest enemies of our people, as well as the greatest threat since many of them were counted among the Elves. Further, the Dark Lord has gained control over the Ogres. How these blood thirsty creatures have come to be ruled by anything but their lust for blood can only be guessed.

"If we do not aid the humans in this fight, it will come directly to our doorstep next. It would only be a matter of time before they broke through our defenses. You all remember the losses we suffered during The War of the Races. We have not seen war since those dark days, and I don't wish for it to come to our home.

"Janeal, I need you to head the council in preparing our forces. We will keep a quarter of our army here, in case the forces are too strong, and we have to fall back to here. I want the most skilled and experienced fighters to come with us."

A woman directly across from Jerech nodded.

"Rioridan, you and Arilie will head to Hindling and seek out the dwarf, Dorin Hamber. Raza knows the way, and is a great friend of theirs. He will guide you there. Once there, tell Dorin we ride to Myrinas to battle, and that we need every dwarf he can manage to rally."

A man and a woman next to Janeal nodded in unison.

"There is no more time to waste!" The urgency in Jerech's command was unmistakable, "The rest of you will take your orders from Janeal. This council is dismissed. I will see you all at Myrinas."

The twelve stood in unison and followed Janeal from the table. The sounds of footsteps faded away and were cut short as soon as the doors closed. Jerech, Jason, Tanas, and Gaibian were all that remained in the room. The orbs started to float above the table, emanating a faint hum.

"These are known as the Orbs of Ojai," Jerech began speaking softly, his face pointed toward the ground.

When he looked up again, his eyes appeared electrified. "In them resides an immense power, and a near infinite knowledge. Every piece of history is recorded in them. Each inhabitant of this planet is accounted for, all the way down to each grain of sand."

The orbs began to glow brighter and circle around the tops of their heads.

The humming seemed to grow louder, but it did not

drown out Jerech's words as he continued, "The orbs were entrusted to me by an ancient ally known as Bahamut, and were delivered here many years ago by Akarah. The only words he left with me were: 'You now hold Myriad in your hands. Protect this gift as you would the most precious thing in your life.'

"The first four were created by the Angel Ojai from water, air, fire, and earth. When he was murdered by his eldest son, not the dragons as was believed, Ojai became the fifth and they were taken by the great dragon Bahamut. He died protecting Akarah, and became the sixth. 'Four from the elements that make up life. One by the blood spilt by betrayal. One for a gesture of love of an enemy. One to know all things from the beginning to the end.'

"When I received the orbs, I did not know what significance they held. It took me ten years before I finally knew exactly what they were, and how to begin to use them. I spent the next six years studying their mysterious power, and learning how to harvest the knowledge they held inside them. It is because of the orbs' warning I sent Jason to Earth, and Akarah remains hidden."

Jerech's eyes looked at each person in turn, seemingly piercing their souls. Electricity flashed in his eyes like bolts of lightning. The orbs now encircled the four men completely. They rose up into the air and the orbs began flying erratically all around them. The same lightning that flashed inside Jerech's eyes flashed inside the orbs.

"It is because of the orbs, Tanas, that Seth was raised and trained by your father."

Jerech reached out his hand, and the orbs came to a sudden stop. The six orbs floated a perfect circle around them, suspending the group in the air. The glow of the orbs hid the ceiling, walls and floor from view.

Jerech's hand remained outstretched as one of the orbs from the circle moved directly in the center. "There is nothing the orbs miss. If a war is fought, a young man wed, or even a child sneezes, the orbs record it. Never has a power been known that could cause the orbs to look away from any event, until the Dark Lord's rise. There lives an evil so powerful it can fool the orbs into thinking nothing around it was happening."

The orb in the middle of them began to expand. All but Jerech feared it would become too large and knock them to the ground. They were so entranced by something inside the orb, however, that they were frozen in place.

Something was happening inside the orb and soon they were each enveloped by it, witnessing something taking place.

A hooded man in a dark cloak leaned over a piece of parchment and wrote furiously. His face was shrouded by the hood, and only his glowing red eyes could be seen. It was the Dark Lord; the man that had caused so much darkness, done so many evil deeds.

Anger welled up inside the prophet's chest. This man had killed his mother so many years ago. Tanas wanted so badly destroy him.

Just as he was about to lash out, Jerech began to speak again, "I know you are angry Prophet, but you must calm yourself. The Dark Lord has destroyed so many lives. Thousands of souls filled with fear bow down at his feet, hoping they might live to see another day. He has perfected a dark magic that makes him invisible to the orbs. Only once since perfecting that power have the orbs seen him."

A horrific battle was being fought. The Dark Lord's forces swarmed through the streets of Myrinas, burning everything and killing anyone who stood in their path. The Dark Lord marched triumphantly toward the center of the city. Victory was nearly at hand. The Oracle stepped out of the temple and stopped at the top of the steps. Her entire body was encased by light. The Dark Lord let out a shrill laugh at the sight of her standing against him. Darkness began to close in around everything as he stepped closer to the Oracle.

"I am Saedin," her voice rang over the sounds of the ward, "the protector of all of Myriad, and as long as there is a breath in my body, you shall not sit upon the throne of Myrinas."

Saedin raised her hands above her head. The light around her body began to intensify, overpowering the darkness. In an instant, the light exploded over the whole of the battle. The Dark Lord's forces were destroyed. The Oracle's hands fell to her sides and she collapsed on the top of the stairs. The Dark Lord, however, had not been destroyed. With his power nearly depleted, he climbed the stairway and grabbed hold of the unconscious Oracle. Everything turned black and the group once again outside the orbs.

"The Dark Lord did not have enough power to take control of Myrinas," Jerech said, "He barely had enough power to take the Oracle away, and to flee into hiding."

Anger began to grow inside the prophet again at the thought of the countless lives that had been lost at evil's hand.

"Quell your anger, Tanas," Jerech's voice grew commanding. "You must listen carefully. You have to understand everything."

The orbs began to circle around them again as they slowly descended back toward the ground.

"The Dark Lord," Jerech continued, "has mastered many powers we still do not know of. You must understand, Tanas, the Dark Lord's most vile act was killing your mother."

As Jerech continued, Tanas couldn't believe all that was being said to him. The evils the Dark Lord had done all centered on the death of his mother, but he could not see how. More anger burned inside him as he remembered watching his mother killed by the Dark Lord's hand as she tried to stop his rampage on Myrinas. As the memory played out in his mind, it played out in each of the orbs.

Tanas knelt, weeping, at his mother's lifeless body. As he looked up into the Dark Lord's eyes, he saw something in them he had never recognized all the times he had dreamed of this moment. Inside the Dark Lord's eyes were sorrow and regret. The shadowed face became clear to Tanas for the first time. The prophet finally knew who the Dark Lord really was.

He could not believe he had never realized the truth of what had happened that day. Tanas still could barely believe it as the true name of the Dark Lord was spoken by Jerech. The four me were set gently back where they had been sitting before. The orbs landed back on the table and went silent.

"How could this have happened?" Tanas asked, dreading the answer.

"We are not completely certain," Jerech answered, "but we believe it had to do with his study of dark magic, and all the research he did on the Dark Alliance. It may have been his intention from the first day he discovered the powers held when in control of Myrinas."

What Tanas had thought had been murder, out of blood lust, had turned out to be accidental, out of carelessness. His mother should have never died that day. The Dark Lord had to pay for his deeds. There was no time to waste. The prophet stood up and threw open the doors to the chamber. He ignored the calls as both Jerech and Gaibian tried to stop him from leaving, but it was too late. Tanas had only one thought on his mind: find and destroy the Dark Lord. He left the castle and went straight to the stables. He mounted a horse and raced out of Midlothian towards Myrinas, stopping for nothing.

7

Reunited

Jason wondered if he should have tried following the prophet as he sat alone in the empty council room. He looked at the orbs on the table. Very little light came from them now. Undistinguishable whispers seemed to be coming from the orbs. Without realizing it, Jason had stretched his hand out for the orb closest to him. The surface felt smooth, like glass. It was warm, like touching something living; he felt the light pulsate as if it had a heartbeat.

Images flashed in his mind. *A beautiful woman and the Elf, Jerech, carrying a bundle through the darkened streets of Keash. They placed it on a door step, tears falling from the woman's eyes. The bundle was a baby.*

The scene changed. *Jason was running ahead of Kristine to the caves they loved.* Everything that had happened since then moved through his mind in an instant up to the moment he had touched the orb. Jason once again saw his dream of Kristine in the prison calling out to him. He pulled his hand away panting. His heart was beating furiously.

"It does take some getting used to," Jerech's voice startled Jason. He was standing with Gaibian behind him, looking slightly amused.

"Come with me, Jason. It is late." Jerech turned and waited, "I have had a room prepared for you, and a meal will be brought to you." Jason stood and followed his father from the room.

"Why didn't you keep me here?" Jason asked.

Jerech did not look at his son, "Your life was in too much danger. It was important to this world - not just your mother and me - that you survive. You have a purpose here far greater than any of us understands. Even what the orbs foretell is hard to decipher."

Jason thought about this a moment and laughed. "Everyone has the same answer. I don't understand how I could possibly save an entire world when I don't know anything."

"Neither do I, my son," Jerech smiled, "But I have found that the answers come to us just as we need them."

He led Jason into a room. A large feather bed sat near an archway leading to a balcony that faced east. No moon shone on this night.

"You are welcome to anything you wish, Jason," Jerech said.

Jason nodded. The amber eyes of Jerech seemed to glisten as he looked at his son.

The Elven king smiled again, "Soreilia will make sure you are taken care of. It has been a long day for all of us; I must retire."

Jerech walked from the room, looking weaker than he had since posing as Orin days before. Gaibian followed after without saying a word, and closing the door behind him. Jason collapsed on the bed and shut his eyes.

After what felt like only seconds, a young Elven woman entered the room carrying a tray full of meat, fruit, and nuts. Jason sat back up, rubbing his eyes.

"Oh! I'm sorry, Sire," Soreilia bowed, "I was told to bring you some food."

"Yeah, uh, thanks. Wait, *Sire*?" Jason replied, not looking up at her.

"Yes. You are the King's son, aren't you?" she asked.

Jason laughed lightly, "I guess I am. You don't need to call me that. Just call me Jason," he looked up at Soreilia for the first time.

She walked noiselessly to Jason and placed the tray next to him. Soreilia's long black hair hung forward on her shoulders, hiding most of her face. Her lavender eyes blended with her deep purple skin. Everything about her movements was smooth, like a dance, and never caused a single sound. Of all the people in this land he had seen so far, Jason thought Soreilia's beauty surpassed that of the others. The only thing about her that matched her beauty was her shyness.

Soreilia bowed again, "I am sorry, Prince Jason. Is there anything else I can get you?"

Jason laughed again, "Just Jason. Do you think you could get me a few extra sheets? It feels like it might get cold."

She smiled at him and nodded, then moved swiftly

from the room. Jason ate while he waited.

When she returned, Soreilia was holding three black sheets.

"Thanks," Jason said as she placed them on the bed next to the tray.

"You're welcome, Si-," she stopped herself and smiled, "You're welcome, Jason. Anything else?"

"No," He said. Soreilia turned to leave when Jason stopped her. "Wait, there is one more thing. Where is this fortress I keep hearing about? Shir- something."

"Shirauk," she replied, "It is to the west. If you follow the river, it will lead you to the mountains, and the canyon that runs through it. It is somewhere in the mountains there."

"Thanks," Jason said thoughtfully, "I'll let you know if I need anything else."

Soreilia left with another nod.

Jason waited for an hour to be sure no one else would come. As soon as he was certain, he decided to move. Using one of the sheets, he dumped the tray into it and wrapped the food up. He strapped the sword that had been left for him to his back. He tied the sheet like a sack and hung it over his shoulder. Next, he tightly tied the remaining sheets together, creating a long rope. He walked to the balcony and tied it tightly to the stone railing, then tossed it over the edge. It barely passed the top of the cliff below. Checking one last time that no one would come in, he started the climb down the sheets.

Jason reached the cliff and climbed a little way down to be sure he was out of sight. He smiled triumphantly and began shimmying sideways along the cliff, nearly slipping several times while looking for hand and footholds. It took him what seemed like another hour before passing the outer wall. He climbed back up over the top of the cliff, panting. Once he had caught his breath, Jason followed the cliff south. He never strayed too far from the cliff edge to be sure he went in the right direction, but never getting too close to be sure he didn't accidentally step over the edge. Several hours later, he heard the sound of the waterfall and ran the remaining distance to the river, feeling very excited.

His triumph spurred him to continue on. He continued west, up along the river. The drive he had was soon diminishing as he thought of the bridge; the only river crossing he knew of. The thought fell from his mind when he was certain he heard something. He shook it off, *how could anything be heard over sound the river?* It did not go away. What he thought he had heard returned. This time, he realized the sound was more like a feeling inside him. It tingled through his whole body, making him tense. Something was wrong. He reached for his sword, but before he could unsheathe it, he once again found himself on his back with a blade to his throat.

"You make enough noise to wake the dead, kid," Gaibian said.

Jason stared up at the black eyes, "Come to finish me off, now that I'm alone?"

"You really are a fool," Gaibian scowled, "You're father sent me to keep an eye on you. You really think he didn't know you would leave?"

Gaibian stood up and reached a hand out to help Jason up. Jason ignored the hand and got back to his feet on his own.

"If he knew," Jason said, "Why didn't he try to stop me?"

Gaibian thought a moment before replying, "Because it is not for him to decide the course you take. Your destiny here is too great to be seen."

"Great, so tell me something I don't already know."

"What you did before you were on your back, that tingle you felt inside you, is a skill that only those with Elven blood can do. It is our ability to hear, and if you can hone it, you will even be able to hear a heart beat from anywhere in the world."

"Right, you expect me to believe that just by focusing I can hear whatever I want, anywhere in the world?"

"How do you explain how I found you so easily?"

"Fine, you found me, now what happens?"

"Now I teach you. You can move over the land or hide in it. You can fight with the land, it will guide you. But what I expect is most important to you is finding your Kristine, and I will take you to her."

"Fine, show me how to get to her, and I'll listen to what you have to teach me." Jason began walking but stopped when he realized Gaibian hadn't moved.

He turned and saw the Elf smiling broadly at him.

"What?" Jason asked.

"You just remind me of a lot of your father," Gaibian replied. "Now, I need you to focus on every sound around us. You need to learn to single out sound in the middle of noise. This will be one of your greatest allies."

Gaibian started walking, and Jason followed behind, trying to concentrate on each sound around him. He found it very difficult to hear anything but the roar of the river.

Just as the bridge came into view he was finally able to *hear* each footstep of Gaibian's, as well encouraging words spoken by the Elf.

"Now is your first real test," Gaibian said. "I need you to find each archer we have stationed here."

Jason closed his eyes as he tried to pick out sound from within the towers. At first, all he heard was one heart beat: his own. Then two; Gaibian was standing directly behind him. Then three and four and it kept going until he could recognize three hundred separate heart beats inside the towers. The sound reverberated inside him.

He opened his eyes and turned around, "I did it. I could hear each of the three hundred elves!"

"Good," Gaibian congratulated him, "Now we walk across the bridge. This time, walk over the moss and not on it."

"Wait," Jason said as Gaibian began walking.

"Is there a problem young prince?" Gaibian's voice was mocking.

Jason scoffed, "How do you expect me to 'walk over the moss and not on it'? What does that even mean?"

"You seemed to catch on so quickly and wish to do so much on your own, I though you knew," Gaibian mocked again.

Jason glared at the Elf.

Gaibian smiled back, "It's a matter of focus and working with the land. It is how all the things we as Elves can do are made possible. You need to allow yourself to trust the land and let it carry you."

Jason stepped forward, and as he did, he felt somehow lighter. It was as if the burden of his weight was being taken on by someone else. He stepped on to the bridge and did not slip. As he neared the other side of the bridge, his confidence rose and he walked faster. The moment he did this, he slipped and fell hard on his back.

Gaibian laughed, "Well, obviously you are as cocky as your father was when he was your age. Get past that and we may survive this journey yet."

Jason got back up and finished crossing the bridge, scowling.

The sun rose, and the air soon became hot and humid. As they traveled on, Gaibian continued testing Jason. He kept trying to teach Jason to focus; usually having him repeat everything he was told.

Near the middle of the day, Jason lost his patience and stopped, "I have to eat and rest. We have been doing this all morning, and I'm tired!"

"If that is what you want, then we will do it," Gaibian said, "But once you learn to focus better, this journey will be much easier on you. Your burden will be lighter."

An hour was allowed to Jason before being told it was time to continue on.

The same tests continued the rest of the day, and late into the night, before Jason collapsed from exhaustion. He crawled to the river and removed his boots to find his feet where blistered and bleeding.

"How much more of this do I have to take?" Jason asked, more to himself than Gaibian.

Even so, a reply was given, "When your father was younger, he too had difficulty connecting with the land. We would set out on marches across many miles and were given no rest for days. When we would finally get to stop, he would go to the river alone and soak his feet, like you are doing now.

"The next morning he would push on, not saying a word of the pain he felt in his feet; never complaining of the aches he felt in his body. He just kept walking. One night, I decided to follow him. He sat on the bank of the river, and I saw him crying. I found it curious that your father, a prince, would cry openly like this. It was then I realized he was talking. I saw no one around; he was talking to Myriad. He kept apologizing for every one of his people that would make her carry them. Jerech told her that he refused to make her carry him too.

"I stepped out from behind the tree that hid me. He was startled by appearance and stood up. His feet were completely healed. I asked him how it was possible. He said she talked to him, told him everything was all right. Then he said something I will never forget, *'She does not hurt the way we do. Because of our love and care for her, she wants to carry us as long as we will let her.'* From that time on, he let her carry him, and Jerech moved quicker and lighter than any of the rest of us."

Jason stared into the river. The cold water eased the pain in his feet. He thought of Kristine and how much easier it would be to get to her if it weren't so difficult to keep up with the elf. Even though he could use the same abilities as they could, everything about him was still so human. But then, it was supposed to just be a dream - yet everything felt so real. So maybe he wouldn't master these things like his father could but he knew one thing for sure, if he could learn to keep doing this one thing, they may not have to stop before reaching Kristine. He fell asleep near the river.

He was flying over this strange new land. Everything was so colorful and beautiful. He rushed through the warm air and landed at a fountain where Kristine sat waiting. She smiled at him and stretched out her hand. He reached his hand toward her. Before he reached her, he felt a sharp stab in his back.

Jason woke up to find he had rolled over onto a sharp rock. He cursed loudly and rubbed his back. The leather had kept him from getting cut, though the pain was still there. Gaibian sat away from Jason, meditating. Once he had noticed Jason was awake, he got quickly to his feet. After a small meal of jerky and berries, they retied their packs and swords to their backs and were off.

Jason was surprised to find today's journey far easier than the previous day. Occasionally he would sip from his water pouch, but they did not stop. All the while, he concentrated to try to single out any sounds around him. Gaibian glanced back from time to time and was quite pleased to see the boy keeping pace with him.

Late into the night they journeyed on. The rocks began to grow darker. The sky seemed to agree this was no place for light. Clouds covered every inch to be sure the sun would not break through. It wasn't long before they reached the mouth of a canyon, and Gaibian signaled to stop.

"This is where things get difficult, prince," Gaibian's

whisper was barely audible, "The things I have taught you become most important here. Even with me, you will not be welcome. I will guide you into the fortress and direct you where to go. After which you must get the Oracle and leave this place as quickly as possible. Be very careful you are not seen. If the Dark Lord sees you, he will kill you without asking questions, so you must not stall for anything. Take her straight to Myrinas. The land will show you the way. Do you understand?"

Jason nodded.

Gaibian pulled two black cloaks from his bag and handed one to Jason. They put them on over their clothes and pulled the hoods over their heads. Jason followed closely behind Gaibian as they climbed the steep pathway. They reached the top without seeing another soul and continued on through a wide ravine. It was obviously man-made by how smooth the walls were. At the end of the ravine they crossed a bridge much wider than the one in the Elven woods. Still, not a soul could be seen around them.

They stepped inside the walls. Everything was black. The entire city was in shambles. It looked as if the dwellings had been torn apart. The two travelers continued on, using the left over debris as cover and avoiding the main road. At the end of the road was a fortress, cut directly from the obsidian mountain. Jason was in awe at the site. They had nearly reached the fortress and still, they met no one. The entire city was deserted. Gaibian had a bad feeling about this; it was all too easy. He expected an ambush at any moment. Perhaps it would come when Jason tried to escape with the Oracle.

Jason followed Gaibian silently into the fortress, and up a long set of stairs. When the stairs broke into two directions, they stopped.

Gaibian whispered even softer than before, "Follow the steps to the right all the way to the top; you might find guards that you will have to kill. I must go the other way to draw any attention from you as you leave. I will turn the Dark Lord's gaze elsewhere. I pray we meet again." The Elf vanished up the stairs to the left.

Jason took the stairs quietly to the right. He listened carefully, just as he had been taught. Adrenaline pumped through his body. He could feel her so close to him; he could hear her cries. Stopping for a moment he listened. The air moved up the stairway. There was only one way in, and one way out of this tower. He had just a few more steps before reaching Kristine. Outside the door, he heard someone breathing. Their heart rate was slow, their breathing even. Whoever was there had fallen asleep. Jason slowly eased his sword from the sheath. He had to be quick.

Pulling his sword back, he dashed around the corner and thrust the blade forward. It slipped easily in and out of the large man sitting in front of the wooden door. He opened his eyes wide then fell over, dead. Jason gulped as he realized he had just killed someone. He shook it off quickly and grabbed the keys that were on the guard's belt. With luck, the first key he pushed in the hole worked. He turned the key and heard the click. Jason pulled the cell door open. There, sitting in the corner and crying, was Kristine Simmons.

Jason put his sword back in the sheath and ran to her.

She looked up at him weakly. "Jason?"

"Yes, I'm here. I came to save you," Jason held her in his arms. "I'm so tired," she said, "I haven't been able to sleep, and they don't give me much food. I don't think I can walk."

"Then I'll carry you," and as he said that he picked

her up and began carrying her down the stairs.

It seemed as though Gaibian's kept his word to keep the pathway clear. They met no resistance all the way out of the fortress. The obsidian city remained quiet and deserted. Jason walked on with only one thought: get Kristine as far away from this place as possible. She dropped off to sleep in his arms when they reached the far side of stone bridge. He forged on. Jason thought nothing of his own desire to rest, or of the hunger he felt in the pit of his stomach. He had to push all this aside until he knew she was safe.

The next morning he couldn't get Kristine to open her eyes. He could barely get her to drink. Her body was very warm, and sweat fell from her forehead. Jason wondered when the fever had broken and hoped that she would get better. He tried getting her to eat some of the fruit he had left, but she vomited it back up shortly after swallowing it. For now, the water would have to do, and he would have to move more quickly. Though he did not know the way, something told him he just had to ask.

He brushed his hand against the soft earth and whispered gently, "Please, you must show me the way to Myrinas. It's where I'm supposed to take her. They will be able to help her get better."

The wind shifted. Jason picked up Kristine and walked with the wind behind him. Somehow, he knew this was the direction he should take her.

The air was dry, and the sun beat hard on Jason's back, but he refused to stop. When the rain came, he covered Kristine in his cloak and braved the cold of the dark night. All thought of sleep left his mind. All thought of pain through is body forgotten. The life held in Jason's arms was the only life he cared to save.

Jason kept the same pace for several days, always heading in the same direction. He would only stop to let Kristine sip as much water as she could, and to refill the canteen with water. On the fifth day she refused to open her mouth for food. The sixth day she was barely responsive enough to drink water. It was the seventh day that Jason feared he would lose his love.

"Please just hold on a little longer," he pleaded to her over and over again.

The sun was creeping behind the western mountain, when hope filled him, after days of walking. Out of the misty plains, a city exploded into sight. He quickened his pace and soon reached the gates. Guards ran out to meet them.

"What has happened?" one of them asked.

"Please," Jason replied, "She needs help. She's really sick. Take me to someone that can help her. It's very important" Sensing the urgency in his voice, the guards escorted Jason directly to the elders.

"You have returned the Oracle to us, stranger," Ardel, head of the elders said to Jason.

"Yes. Can you please help her?" Jason held his composure the best he could.

"I am afraid," Ardel answered in his squeaky voice, "She has been cursed by the Dark Lord. The only thing I know of to save her may not exist. There is a fabled fountain atop the Misty Mountains that surround us. If it exists, drinking the water directly from the fountain will cure her. If not, it is certain she will die."

Jason fought back the tears, "Then I'll take her there. I won't let her die."

8

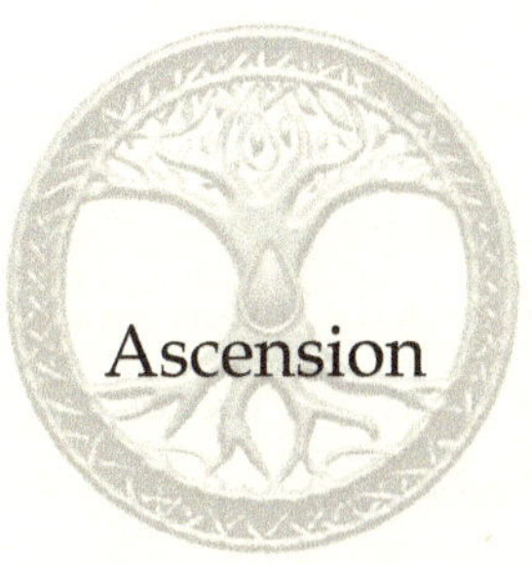

Ascension

Jason wasted no time, though much to the protest of the elders. He had traveled for many days, and it had been more than a week since he had slept for more than a couple hours.

"Please," Ardel pleaded with him, "You must rest. We can buy her some time. Do not kill yourself, it would be foolish."

Jason laughed for the first time in days, "Someone I know liked to remind me I'm a foolish boy."

News had traveled quickly that the Oracle had been brought back to Myrinas by a young man named Jason. The story of his endless quest to save her was retold until everyone had heard. Though much of the detail was missing, each retelling was given a new spin. In everyone's eyes, Jason was now a hero. Though the elders had refused to show Jason the way the way to the mountains, every citizen of Myrinas was willing to guide him.

It seemed that not a single person remained in their homes as Jason began the journey. He was led by several guards back out of the city gates. They followed the base of the mountain several miles. Occasionally, someone would approach him and offer to carry her part of the way.

Jason refused; he felt it was his duty, alone, to carry her all the way. If he had already carried her this far, how much harder could it be to carry her up a mountain?

He asked several people about the mountain pass, before a small boy finally had an answer.

"I've made it the highest," the boy boasted, "It gets really steep, and the ledge gets really thin. I got scared and ran back home."

It seemed that no one had ever reached the top of this mountain. It seemed to Jason this may be a fool's errand. If no one else would try, he had to be the fool to try it. Everything else had been too good to be true, so this had to be, too. If not, she would die anyway. He had to know he had at least tried.

The climb to the summit started out steady and smooth. The burden of Kristine's weight in Jason's arms was barely felt, regardless of the long journey preceding. The sun had broken through the clouds, drying the ground from the rain the day before, and heating up the air. Perspiration fell from Jason, soaking his cloak, and adding to the weight of Kristine's unconscious body in his arms.

Footing became harder to find, making the climb increasingly difficult. The town's people that had been following had stopped trying to keep up, simply watching from below until the travelling stranger was out of sight. New hope had filled everyone when he had arrived with the Oracle. They all felt Jason would be the one to save her, if anyone could.

A narrow ledge and a long fall caused Jason to keep his back to the sharp walls to stay as far from the edge as possible. The adrenaline flowing through him masked the pain from the cuts on his back, though he could feel the blood. The rains did not start up again, and for that Jason was grateful. He knew it would make the climb all the more dangerous when the rocks got slippery and could possibly cause parts of the cliffs to break away. He suppressed a shudder as he pictured the fall.

After hours of climbing, they reached the summit; Kristine's breathing grew fainter. The valley stretched on out of sight. Scars from past wars could be seen throughout the plains. The forests and farms that scattered the land faded off in the distance. A more spectacular sight could not be seen from anywhere Jason had been in his life. He looked at Kristine's quiet face, and knew he had to continue. He pushed on through the tall grass and overgrown brush that hid the broken stone. What would have otherwise been a beautiful walkway was now overgrown chaos from years of abandonment. Kristine's pulse weakened. Jason pushed on faster through the foliage, as quickly as his weary body would allow.

Finally coming to a clearing, Jason came to a sudden stop before reaching a cliff only a few feet away. Two hundred feet below, a river tore through boulders and jagged rocks. On either side of Jason stood statues of angels; a man and a woman holding swords that pointed up. Both were facing in, and appeared to be looking directly at Jason and Kristine, as if in judgment. Hints of a bridge crossing the river remained. Loops on the hilt of the swords showed where ropes had once been tied. Burn marks left no question as to what had happened to the bridge. The statues mirrored on the opposite end, nearly a hundred feet away. Fear, anger, and panic swept over Jason as he looked up and down the river for another way across.

He refused to accept that he had reached an end. There was still a chance to save her. He gently laid her down on a shady patch of grass, and then sat, cross-legged, on the edge of the cliff. Calm settled over him as he closed his eyes, searching for an answer. He focused on the land around him, listening for any sound holding an answer. Time seemed to be at a complete standstill. The world seemed to fall silent. He knew swimming across would not work. Even if the climb were possible, the river would sweep them both away. There was no time, nor means, to try to build a bridge. There was a way, and Jason would find it.

Jason opened his eyes and slowly lifted his head. He felt as if he were being watched from across the river. Out of the shadows a bird flew toward him. Each beat of its wings seemed to match Jason's heart. As the sun hit the bird, he could see the beauty of its blue and white feathers. Stripes of black intermixed on its wings and tail, and two crossed its chest in the shape of a 'V'. It stared meaningfully at him as it reached the mid-point and looked like it was trying to land.

The heavy sound of stone grinding flooded Jason's ears, and shock filled his whole body as the bird landed gracefully on a block, where before there at been only air. Still looking at Jason, the blue jay blinked once, then took off in flight, again as the stone fell beneath it and the bird headed toward the blinding sun to the west. The answer was now very clear, and he was certain his plan would work. He carefully picked up Kristine and carried her to the edge. He took a deep breath and stepped out into nothing.

His foot came down harder than he had intended, causing him to nearly lose his balance and drop Kristine. Jason fell forward onto his knees and landed on another stone that appeared. He felt the ache as his body took the shock of the fall. He could feel the stone he had just been standing on falling behind him, leaving his feet hanging in the air.

He stood up, wincing from the new pain in his knees. Stones slowly began to appear in front of him across the air. This meant only one thing: he didn't have much time before they, too, would fall, and he and Kristine would follow.

He leapt on to the next stone just as the one he

had been on dropped. Using this momentum, Jason began running as fast as he could, the stones behind him falling just after he landed on the next. The end felt miles away. Jason did not stop on the other side after leaving the enchanted bridge, but kept running on.

The trees and bushes on both sides, though still consuming the pathway, were so much more alive on this side of the chasm. There was a reverence emanating from them. It was as if they were showing respect to the Oracle, and guiding the way. Jason's movement through was easy. Cool air surrounded him. The brush seemed to move out of his way. *It had to be the wind,* he thought. Nothing else before this had been nearly this easy. The trees overhead kept them both shaded. The pathway winded back and forth through what appeared to have been gardens. Several pathways branched off, but in following the way the plants were moving, Jason kept on what he knew was the main path. Though hard to believe, Jason imagined the already breathtaking beauty of this place was once so much more, when taken care of.

A clearing soon appeared ahead. He could hear the soft trickling of water. A magnificent city burst into view as he broke through the last of the trees. The colors had clearly faded, and vines had made their home on anything they could, but the buildings all seemed in perfect order. Time and nature had not cracked or destroyed a single building. Whatever had happened, wherever the people had gone to, no sign remained to answer those questions.

Jason's eyes stopped on a fountain in the middle of it all. Seven stone angels, three women and four men, stood evenly spaced in a circle facing the fountain. Their heads were slightly bowed, and there seemed to be reverence carved into their faces. Between each of the statues, small and fierce dragon heads protruded from the fountain. Out of their mouths flowed crystal clear water from the fountain and into streams traveling all over the city. There were eight serpents, in all. This was where he had to go. Kristine had to have the water from this fountain.

Though he didn't see why this would be different from any place else, it somehow felt significant. As impossible as it seemed, this was the most real any of this adventure felt since Jason had arrived on Myriad. Right now, holding *her* in his arms as he approached the fountain. Everything else could be a dream as, long as he still had this.

A few feet short of the fountain, Jason halted

suddenly. A sharp pain coursed through his body. He looked down and saw a blade coming out of his chest, just missing Kristine. His body jerked back as the blade was pulled out. He stumbled forward and fell, once again, on his already bruised and bleeding knees.

He felt his elbows crack as they connected with the edge of the fountain. Kristine rolled out of his arms and fell into it, causing the still water to splash over the edges. Her head shot up instantly out of the water, and she sucked in a deep breath of air. Jason looked up, and for the first time since he got here, locked eyes with the girl he would never stop loving. He smiled caringly at her and fell weakly to the ground.

"No!" Kristine screamed as jumped out of the fountain. She cradled Jason in her arms and held him, trying to slow the blood that fell freely from his wounds. All these years she had ached to hold him, and now he was finally here. Tears slowly came to her eyes.

As they tenderly held each other, both felt as if it was the end of their love story that had just begun. She cried into his chest, feeling his heart slowing with each beat. The flow of the blood had nearly stopped. His skin grew pale. Jason pulled Kristine away from him, and they locked eyes. There was no pain, only happiness, as he stared deep in her eyes. He had saved her, and that was all that mattered to him now.

Behind them, Seth stood in shock as the Dark Lord's controlling spell had been broken. Fear and remorse filled his entire being. The bloody sword was held loosely at his side. As he saw Jason's face, the realization of his actions seemed to steal the air from his lungs. His heart told him this young man was more than just a stranger. He had just murdered his brother.

He dropped to his knees, letting go of the sword. The clanging of the metal seemed to vibrate through his body. He watched as the two gazed into each others' eyes. The bind that had once tied him so strongly to the Dark Lord had been broken, and so had his soul.

"What have I done?" The words tasted like venom escaping his lips. Out of the shadows, a dark figure silently approached Seth. A cold gray hand came down softly on Seth's shoulder.

"Do not mourn, my young prince," the voice was low and raspy. The words were slow and drawn out.

Seth looked up at the hooded figure with tears

forming in his eyes. The man, if you could call him that, had gray skin and very white hair. He did not look like he was alive, nor did he look dead, though his skin was heavily deteriorated. Something about this *man* seemed somehow familiar to Seth as well, and he felt like they had seen each other before.

"Your brother is not dead. This has all just been a bad dream. I can show you the way out, Prince. I will help you to end this nightmare and make everything right again. Just come with me and my master will make everything right. Draedin has greater power than the Dark Lord you serve." One of the decaying hands gestured out of his cloak toward a walkway that disappeared into darkness. Seth stood hesitantly and started to walk, stopping to look back one last time at his dying brother before vanishing into the brush.

"I have never stopped searching for you," Jason's voice was very weak.

"Please, try not to talk. Save your strength. There has to be a way to save you," Kristine tried to look brave, but the tears flowing freely from her eyes revealed the truth.

"I came here looking for you; I came to save you. Now you are safe, and everything will be all right for you." Jason tried to lift himself up.

Kristine, reading his eyes, leaned down and met his lips with the embrace she had always longed for. They held the kiss as long as Jason had strength to hold himself up. He moaned as he settled back in her lap.

"There is one thing I have to tell you before I go." His eyes burned deep into hers, "I- I lo-"

The words never came. Jason winced heavily as the pain shot through his body, making him unable to speak. He exhaled one last time, and fell limp.

Kristine leaned over onto his chest, crying, never able to hear the words she had waited all these long years for. Just to hear him say that he loved her, and being able to say she loved him too. The sun fell beneath the horizon. The warm water from the various streams began to rise around them. Jason's body was picked up and started floating away from Kristine. She cried as she watched, feeling that she must not try to stop it; feeling helpless for the life that fate had stolen from her once again. She didn't move until his body fell over the edge of the cliff out of view.

9

Call to Arms

The deed is done my Lord." Though he had spent many years in his service, Gaibian still feared laying his eyes on the Dark Lord.

"Excellent. The Oracle is right where I need her to be, and soon no obstacle will stand in my way of taking over Myrinas. I will be returning there soon. Now, where is my other faithful general?" The Dark Lord's eyes glowed blood red. His face had become dull grey and sunken from his long years of living in darkness and evil. His entire being, clear through to his heart had grown as cold as ice, and it was reflected in his voice.

"I am afraid, my Lord," Gaibian began repentantly, "he will not be returning." A cold chill crept slowly up Gaibian's spine. His hot breath could be seen in the air.

The Dark Lord stood still on the balcony, overlooking Shirauk's remains. The door behind Gaibian opened and a young girl entered carrying a tray with food for the Dark Lord. The cold spread to Gaibian's legs. They grew numb, and he was unable to move.

"So many faithful and obedient followers out there, Gaibian. So many souls that are easily replaced, if I see fit to dispose of a weak link; to destroy an anomaly."

The young girl set the tray on a table and filled a goblet with wine, then proceeded to make the bed, ignoring the words of her master. She had grown used to his temper in the few weeks she had been assigned to prepare his meals and clean his spacious room. She admired the rug that lay beneath the oversized four poster bed. It was a comfort to walk on something as soft and warm as this, since she had to work barefoot, and the obsidian was hard and cold. She would occasionally glance up at the Elf that served her master, admiring him from afar. He seemed so much warmer and brighter than everything else here. It was nice to see a smile as he would pass her.

His face was more distraught today than others. He seemed to be in pain, though there were no physical signs.

"There are however," the Dark Lord's voice grew colder and angrier, "those that are irreplaceable, and it would be in the best interest of some to make sure those assets always return!"

An icy wind blew across the room. The girl stood up in shock and was frozen, encased in a block of ice.

The Dark Lord's voice lowered, "Have this girl put with the others. Find me one that is not so pathetic to fall in love you." Gaibian started for the doorway to call for the guard, "And Gaibian." He stopped halfway through the door and looked back as his master spoke to him, "My armies are now in place. Do not come to me again until we have taken Myrinas."

As Gaibian closed the door behind him, he heard the shrill laughter of the one man he truly feared, and the one man he could not leave under strict orders from Jerech.

There was no time left to waste. The Dark Lord was getting ready to move his armies closer to Myrinas, and word needed to spread quickly. When he was sure he was out of sight, he jumped through a window, changing instantly into a blue jay once more, and flew off into the pitch, silent night.

This form was always his favorite. Being high above everything and being able to see the world from this perspective was unbelievable. The feel of air rushing around him as he dove and glided through the endless sky left him elated. And by far, this was the quickest way to scout and travel without detection. Even the Dark Lord didn't know of Gaibian's ability to change. The thought would have made him smile, if he wasn't a bird. He knew his next stop; he had to fly deep into the forest and report to Jerech immediately. He also wanted answers.

Gaibian had trailed off in thought so far that he was already deep in the trees before he realized he had left the open air. He wove easily through the tall trees, watching and listening for any animals that might mistake him for dinner. Not far off he could hear voices talking lightly. News of the death of the prince had not yet arrived in Midlothian.

He found the balcony to Jerech's chamber. The change back to human was just as quick as the change to a bird as he landed noiselessly at the door.

"You're late." The deep, stern voice came from behind thick curtains, slightly startling Gaibian. He had never gotten used to Jerech knowing exactly the moment of his arrival, even though Jerech was one of the very few who knew Gaibian could change. "So, what news, my old friend?" Jerech's voice was instantly friendly and inviting.

"I am still trying to understand the reason you would allow me to lead Jason all that way, only to be killed by his twin brother!" Gaibian's tone exposed more anger than intended.

"There is still much about this even I don't understand." The king let out a heavy sigh, "All I know is that this is the only hope we have of defeating the Dark Lord for good." Jerech's eyes looked heavy in concentration. "I am unable to see beyond that. There is…a block."

"But how is it possible, if the one person strong enough to defeat him is dead?"

"I cannot say I understand it myself. We just have to accept that there are stronger forces at work here. A power greater than any we have ever experienced before. A power that is so great, not even the Orbs can see the motivating force behind the inevitability of it." Jerech sagged into his chair.

"Pardon me, Sire, but I have brought you your supper." Gaibian's head turned to the sound of the soft, feminine voice that had interrupted the conversation. Her head was slightly bowed, and her short, dark hair covered most of her face. Her beautiful Elvish features hit Gaibian's eyes, stopping his breath momentarily. She nearly bumped into Gaibian before noticing him. She stuttered apologetically, "Excuse me, Sire, I did not realize you had a guest. I shall fetch him supper as well."

"Thank you, Soreilia," Jerech replied, smiling at her as he would his own daughter. She whisked out of the room without so much as disturbing the dust on the floor, slightly flushed at the obvious attention from her king's guest.

Jerech waited a moment before speaking, "Gaibian, if you are through, I believe you had other matters to discuss with me than the death of my son." The mocking in Jerech's voice pulled Gaibian's attention back to the matter at hand. Gaibian sat in a chair next to the king's. He felt drained from all that had happened.

"Everything we feared about the Dark Lord taking over is happening now," Gaibian said. "It seems Tanas will soon return to Myrinas to speak with Silamond. The Prophet is angry; more than we could imagine. The Dark Lord is pleased by this. He says it will make everything far easier. The whole of his army is stationed throughout the woods bordering the planes. They wait until the Dark Lord gives the signal for them to move. I have not yet been able to get the exact meaning behind what he says. It's so shrouded. You should also know that Seth has vanished"

Jerech nodded, "You have done well, my friend. I will not ask you to return to the Dark Lord again. The final assault must take place soon. We still have no word from the Dwarfs. I hope Rioridan and Arilie can find them soon. We have other friends deeper in the woods that may be able to help. This is where I need you now, Gaibian.

"There is a place even deeper in the woods than Midlothian where twilight is ever present; a place where all remains green and life flourishes. It is called Twilight's Grove, and it is in this place you will find the children of Myriad."

Gaibian tried to feign shock, "Why me?"

"You can't hide everything from me, old friend. I know it is because of them you were able to achieve your ability to change. There is nothing dark about the way you do this."

"Your wisdom is impressive, as always,"

Gaibian thought of the orbs, "How did you come by this knowledge?"

"Yes, it is through *them* that I know. It is also how I know you must be the one to go."

"How much do you rely on the orbs, Jerech? We both know they weren't intended for our use. They were placed in your care to protect them. How much of this would we have if it weren't for their help?"

Jerech looked away, "Just go." Then he added, "Please."

Gaibian left at the king's request.

Jerech was left alone to ponder the extent to which he had used the orbs since receiving them. Though the king did not appear so outwardly, he felt old in his heart. He felt worn from the use of the orbs, and wondered if it was wise to use them again. This was, after all, his intent. He let out a long sigh after deciding it might not be a good idea. Sinking back in his chair, he began to wonder if he had the strength to keep himself from using them.

Gaibian left the city late that night. All his life, Gaibian preferred exploring Myriad to staying behind walls. Remaining too long in any one place only made him feel restless and trapped. It had been years since he had happened on Twilight's Grove.

When he was eight years old he had decided to run away. His mother always insisted he stay inside the city walls so he would be safe. Gaibian did not see the problem; he knew the woods better than most, and he always managed to stay out of trouble; or at least get himself back out of it. The city walls felt too much like a prison to him. After his mother had fallen asleep, he snuck out. Quietly, he made his way out of this city and deep into the woods.

Not long after leaving, he came upon a pack of wolves that were not acting in their nature. The wolves did not move like a hunting pack, but walked casually in a 'V' formation, with the largest at the lead. They looked determined about where they were going. Their eyes always faced forward, and their ears never perked at any sound around them. Something compelled him to follow, staying hidden as much as possible.

Gaibian soon noticed light breaking through the trees. It seemed strange to him that the sun was rising already. Perhaps time had gone by much faster that he thought. The closer they got, the more he realized this was the only place with light. Closer and closer they got; less and less the light appeared to be from the sun. It took until Gaibian could see through the break in the trees to see it opened up into a magnificent grove. It no longer looked like the sun was rising, but setting instead. It was twilight.

Past the trees it opened up into a beautiful grove. Flora blanketed the grove such as Gaibian had never seen before; fauna of all sorts grazed happily. The wolves were nearly to the edge of the grove now. The nostrils of the largest wolf flared. Gaibian shuttered at the thought of the beasts killing the creatures. Still, he was drawn in and could not turn his gaze away. His heart beat with anticipation. The wolves walked behind a large tree out of Gaibian's view. Wolves are not what came out from behind the tree.

They were no longer a pack of wolves but something Gaibian had never seen in his life. Except for the largest that stood twelve feet tall, each of them were close to ten feet; this was only because all of their heads were hunched forward on necks that stretched out from their shoulders about two feet. Their long muscular legs were slightly bent at the knee and their heads bobbed as they walked. They had long sloth-like arms. Long shaggy hair covered their enormous bodies all the way to their necks. On the largest, two bull-like horns curved out in front of its face.

Gaibian's mouth hung open. An uncomfortable feeling

entered his stomach. He backed up without taking his eyes of the large beasts. He bumped into something furry and fell forward. A large hand grabbed him and carried him over to the others.

"Let me go," he wiggled and kicked with all his might to break from the grasp.

He was held up in front of the largest. Its eyes seemed to pierce clear through to Gaibian's soul. He stopped struggling and just stared back. Right before Gaibian's eyes the creature changed. Gaibian blinked, disbelieving what he just saw. It was no longer a beast, but an Elf.

The transformation was so quick and so smooth that no one would believe it had happened if they blinked.

"Who are you, youngling, and what brings you to our home?" there was nothing threatening or angry about the Elf's voice. It was very kind and calming.

"My name is Gaibian," the young Elf answered, "I ran away from home. I didn't mean to cause trouble."

Gaibian felt no need to lie, though he doubted anything else he said would be believable. The older Elf laughed, and all the creatures seemed to laugh as well; it was a very beautiful, uplifting sound as, if it were happiness itself.

"My name is Dalatori, and this," Dalatori gestured, "is Twilight's Grove."

Over the next several years Gaibian stayed with Dalatori and his people. He learned that were an ancient race called the Othniel. They were changelings; though they had not always been that way. It was merely through the need to survive they could change. As Gaibian grew he was taught their history. He learned how they were the literal children of Myriad, and slept only because it was relaxing, not a necessity. Before long, Gaibian was taught to transform.

"But only," Dalatori instructed, "If you promise me to return to your mother directly after, and let her know you are safe and well."

Gaibian nodded in agreement.

Upon mastering the skill, he changed into a blue jay and flew toward his home. He weaved in and out of the trees of the Othnielian woods. Gaibian landed at the door of the home he left four years earlier. He took a deep breath and stepped inside.

His mother lay in bed, very ill. She was barely able to lift her head enough to see her son walk in.

A weak smile came to her face, "I knew you would come home."

Gaibian knelt next to his mother's bed, holding her hand and crying. He laid his head on her stomach, and she ran her fingers through his hair; her other hand still held his tightly. Just as suddenly as the moment had begun, it ended. One last breath escaped her lungs. The boy cried for several hours before carrying her into the woods where his father had been buried. He laid her to rest next to her husband, and then fell asleep near the graves.

He never returned to the Othniel as had been planned.

It all seemed like another life; someone else's life. Since that time Gaibian had tried to blame his mother's death on the Othniel. If they had just told him to go home she wouldn't have gotten sick. She would still be alive. Deep down he knew this to be untrue. It had all been because of his decision to leave home. Wherever the blame stood, Gaibian never wanted to return there. Twilight's Grove was the last place he wanted to go; yet it was where he knew he must go.

Gaibian did not understand the request Jerech was making, nor did he think Jerech knew what he was asking of Gaibian. The Othniel disliked violence and confrontation in any form. It seemed to be a violation of nature to ask the most peaceful race to go to war. For this, Gaibian felt ashamed. There did not seem to be any hope in this campaign. But he would try for his king - for his friend.

It took several days before Gaibian found something familiar to him: a tree that had grown through a rock and split it in half. This had been the last place he hid when following the wolves that turned out to be the Othniel. The woods surrounding the grove appeared darker; they *felt* darker. It seemed as if the clouds never cleared from the sky. Less light from the grove seeped into the Othnielian woods than Gaibian remembered.

The blue jay took flight from where Gaibian had been standing. He flew into the grove, feeling the warmth the shadows of the trees did not hold. Animals all through the Twilight's Grove watched the bird fly through, and changed to their true form as they followed. Over a hundred Othniel stood around the bird that landed before Dalatori. In front of all the witnesses Gaibian changed back to himself. Dalatori's eyes sparkled with delight.

"It's been a while, my friend," Gaibian said.

"Has it?" Dalatori replied, "How long have you been away youngling?"

"You view time differently than we do," answered Gaibian, "so according to our figuring it has been eighty-three years."

"Hmm," Dalatori nodded.

Gaibian took a step toward the leader of the Othniel, "I have come on an errand of great importance, Dalatori. Your kind has never done more than survive. You have been here since the beginning of this world, and witnessed the wars of men. I know it is not in your nature to meddle in the affairs of men, but this is no longer the fight of men alone. The Dark Lord will stop at nothing to control the land, and every living thing in it. He shows no mercy to those who do not swear allegiance to him; man and beast alike. I have come to beg you fight with us."

Dalatori looked from Gaibian to his people and back again. His voice was steady and calm, as always, "You are one of few outsiders that know of our existence here, brother of the Othniel. You know more of our ways than any other. Mother Myriad has always given us what care we need to survive, and shall continue to do so as long as life beats within her. Your time with us still did not teach you this, youngling."

Many nodded in agreement.

The Elf felt foolish. He thought for a moment, and

then turned around, surveying all that was in the grove.

He looked at the sky above, "This is not a matter of my misunderstanding your way of life. You must stand and fight with us for the sake of Myriad; for the sake of your survival."

One of the Othniel spoke, "You have already said we do not fight the wars of men."

Another spoke, "Nor do we involve ourselves with the affairs of men."

And another, "Our life is one of peace. We will not fight."

More and more spoke up in agreement that war was not the answer. The chorus became so loud, yet it was like a song. Gaibian became momentarily stunned by the beauty of it all; so much so that he nearly forgot his purpose in coming.

He shook his head and raised his voice louder, "The darkness is already making its way here. Just look around you!" Gaibian gestured out to the surrounded forest, "Have you not noticed the blight that spreads through your woods? Even the brilliance of your grove has begun to fade."

"Gaibian," Dalatori interjected slightly impatient now, "There is no more to be said here. We will do what we have always done; live in harmony with all living things. No substantial evidence shows we are in any danger. Myriad herself speaks to us. She would warn us if danger were at our doorstep." Several chuckled at Dalatori scolding of the Elf like a child. He raised his hands to bring silence, "Twilight's Grove has always been, and will always be a place of pure serenity. This light will never fade."

Gaibian sighed, turned around, and started walking away as the crowd cleared a path for him. His head hung low as he walked out of the grove and returned to the rock where he had laid his pack down. He grabbed it, testing the weight in his hands. The decision still made him feel a little guilty, but it was the only way. It seemed to Gaibian the right outweighed the wrong. Throwing the bag over his shoulder, he walked slowly back into the grove; the battle in his mind still continued.

"Have you returned to further plea for a lost cause youngling?" Dalatori was surprised to see Gaibian return so quickly.

The Elf felt defeated by what he must do. He dare not look Dalatori in the eyes. Gaibian knelt before the Othniel and placed his pack in front of him. He reached in and found a ball the size of an apple; it felt like glass. After pulling it out he placed it on the ground in front of him. He repeated this five more times placing them in a line. Dalatori watched curiously.

"What?" Dalatori began, but stopped immediately as a faint blue light began to glow in the center of each of the orbs. "How have you come into possession of these, youngling?" Dalatori's whisper was barely heard.

Gaibian answered half-truthfully, "They were given to the care of the Elves. I have brought them to you so you may see what lies ahead. This is the proof you need."

The scene in the grove changed. No longer was there an audience of Othniel watching. No longer was the grove full of life and light.

Mutilated bodies of the Othniel littered the burning grounds. Ogres stood triumphantly over the bodies. None of the magnificent changelings had survived the massacre. The scene played backward. Gaibian and Dalatori watched in reverse as the Othniel were brutally cut down. The Ogres flooded in from the surrounding forest and throwing torches. The darkness overpowered the light. Hundreds of Othniel sitting unaware of what was coming.

Every second passed by until they stood where they had just been moments before. Tears dropped from Dalatori's eyes.

"My dear brothers and sisters," Dalatori's voice boomed, "It is time to call on those not with us. A great evil will destroy us if we do not meet it first."

The command in his voice left none protesting. A beautiful sound, like a lullaby, came from the Othniel. It started very low and soft and gradually grew louder; soon getting so loud Gaibian felt as if it filled his entire body. Several hundred animals walked or flew into Twilight's Grove, changing back into their great race shortly after; each joining in the song.

After the last had arrived, Dalatori spoke very briefly of what was to come, "The mother that has given us life is in danger. For this cause we go to war against those that threaten her."

No more was need to be said by Dalatori. All turned and followed him out of the grove.

10

The Descent

Kristine was left sitting alone; despite the water, she was completely dry. The only thing left was the sword that had ended the life of the man who had saved hers.

She stood in the darkness, facing the cliff, and whispered into the wind, hoping his spirit might hear her, "I love you Jason England."

He really was gone. The tears fell freely from her eyes.

A warm wind wrapped around her, reminding her of Jason's arms. She felt comforted, though she still felt the need to cry. Tears of anger began to mix with tears of grief. Kristine began to feel a familiar fire deep inside her; one that took her back to when it first happened.

Deep in the temple she hid in the corner of her room, afraid, tears falling from her eyes. She knew he was coming. The Dark Lord was coming for her. She had already seen it, but knowing did not make it easier for her.

"Why me?" she asked, "I'm only eighteen years old."

The Prophet Tanas knelt down beside her, "Everyone here is trying to protect you Saedin. They will do everything they can to keep you safe. But you have the power to stop this; you have the power to stop **him.***"*

"Why do you keep calling me 'Saedin'?" she asked, "My name is Kristine. I just want to be Kristine."

"Saedin is always the name given to our Oracle. It means 'Seer and Protector'. It is what you are." Tanas's eyes were very kind and held the care of an older brother in them. Kristine was awed by the power he had for being twenty-seven. She could see it in him. So much of his past was locked away inside. Deeper in she peered, seeing not an hour before when his mother had been killed. Past that, she could see this moment; she saw herself through his eyes. He cared for her like a brother. Shortly after this, there was only darkness. Kristine began to cry again.

The door to her room burst open and her mother ran

through the door. Kristine ran to her and was enfolded in her arms, burying her head in her mother's chest.

"Tanas, we need to hide her somewhere," Kiera was fighting back her emotions, "They are almost through. Johnathan is trying to hold them back, but he doesn't-"

Kiera's body jerked forward and she screamed out in pain. As she started to fall, she twisted to her side to keep from falling on Kristine. The arrow had pierced her heart. She coughed up blood and lay dead.

"Mom?" Kristine shook her mother's body as if to wake her.

"RUN!" a man's voice called from the hallway.

"Daddy," Kristine cried out to her father, "Help! Please, Daddy, save me!"

Tanas tried to pull the girl away from her mother, but she refused to let go.

The sound of steel clashing echoed in the room several times. It was finally broken as the tearing of flesh could be heard by the two left in the room. Johnathan grunted and his body fell back, crashing through the door. He had been stabbed in the stomach. Kristine screamed. Tanas tried to push her behind him, but she would not move.

Johnathan refused to give up. He grunted feeling the pain in his stomach where the steel had pierced him. He held the wound to try to slow the bleeding. He held his sword at the ready for the oncoming Orcs. Kristine screamed as the first came into view. Johnathan deflected the blow that came at him and cut the Orc's throat before he had a chance to recover and attack again.

"Get my daughter out of here, Tanas," he yelled. "Now!"

Tanas went to grab the Oracle, but was unable to move. Something was holding him back. He tried and tried, but nothing he did would allow him to move an inch. He stared at Kristine, bewildered. The air started to move around the girl crying over her mother's body.

A second Orc, much larger than the first, came into the room. He swung an ax at Johnathan's head but the human rolled to the left just in time. The smooth steel of the blade brushed the side of his face. This proved more difficult than Johnathan had planned. The loss of blood had left him dizzy, and he fell off balance. He was able to look at his daughter one last time before the Orc brought the ax down on his skull.

"Stupid humans," the Orc grunted. He removed the ax from his kill and turned his sights on Kristine smiling, "So,

you're the little girl the Dark Lord wants so badly."

Kristine looked up and froze in terror; tears still streamed down her face.

"Leave her alone," Tanas said with a commanding voice, though still unable to move.

The Orc laughed at Tanas and turned back to the girl, "He will be pleased with me."

He was only an arm's length away when he stopped. Confusion replaced triumph. Suddenly, he was thrown back through the door, hitting a wall. Bricks crumbled and fell, crushing the life out of his body.

Tanas stared at the Oracle, now feeling the power emanating from her; the power of every Oracle that lived before her. Kristine stood facing the door.

"Do not leave this room," the voice was no longer that of the frightened eighteen year-old girl, but a resonating choir of strong, beautiful voices. Bright blue flames burst up around her causing her body fall into a dark shadow. The ground beneath her cracked as she walked forward, and the fire rose higher, moving with her.

Kristine had always feared this power; had held it back

not knowing if she could control it. She never understood the power bestowed upon her. Now the anger and grief at her loss buried the fear deep inside her. Vengeance took hold of her and unleashed the power to get rid of this evil.

The fire continued to rise as she walked through the hall. The temple broke apart around her, exploding when the fire had risen higher than the ceiling. The temple remained in shambles, and still Kristine did not look back. All around the temple people she knew and loved were being killed by Orcs, Ogres, harpies, and all manner of dark creatures. Above, the Dark Lord stood on black cloud, shards of ice raining on people below. Whether enemy or ally, he did not care. Bolts of lightning flashed from his fingers, and he laughed at the carnage below.

Kristine spotted him. The anger grew inside her at the evil invading her home; the evil destroying her friends. A ball of the blue fire formed in her hands, and she threw it at the Dark Lord. It hit him square in the chest. He was knocked off the cloud and fell hard to the ground. He stood up, the lightning dancing on his fingers. He shot it at her but the fire around her absorbed it. The flames grew bigger. Again and again he tried as she walked closer to him. The fighting had stopped, and all were watching the two beings of power facing one another.

"Kill them all!" the Dark Lord commanded. His gaze

never left the Oracle as the fighting recommenced.

She had had enough, "No more of your death or evil shall remain here."

Kristine thrust her hands straight out to her side and the fire broke out in all directions killing nearly every follower of the Dark Lord. The Dark Lord himself lay nearly dead in the street, his power drained from him. Those of his followers that remained gathered round him. He pointed to the Oracle who lay unconscious, no longer surrounded by the fire. They grabbed Kristine, and carried the Dark Lord and her from the city before anyone could stop them. They went into hiding, until the Dark Lord could regain power once more.

Kristine blinked. Just as had happened two years ago, the power began to flow around her. It felt more controlled than before. She felt like she could focus the power more. This time she would not fail. This time the Dark Lord would not take her. She dug down deeper in her heart and pulled out every piece of anger and despair she had ever experienced. It was so fresh in her mind, this would be her driving force.

Visions flashed through her mind. The destruction of the Dark Lord by a faceless power. Peace throughout the lands. New life. She must make this happen! She must stop the Dark Lord's evil for good!

She walked to the edge of the cliff that had taken her love. The clouds had settled low. Nothing of Myrinas or the surrounding plains could be seen. She knew the invasion was beginning, and something very evil was ensuing. She turned; her tattered dress billowed in the sudden rush of wind. The covered pathway opened up for her as if it had been waiting for her departure.

As she walked through the pathway, it closed behind her. She was led directly to the enchanted bridge by the plant life. Once at the ledge, she closed her eyes and focused to see what had happened before, to see how they had crossed. Kristine saw everything of Jason's coming here. She saw where he had gone when they separated, saw him come for her and never wavering in his desire to save her. She saw him carry her all the way here, and cross the enchanted bridge. He lay dead, and then she could not see him anymore.

When she opened her eyes she was very aware of a significant change. Three days had passed her by. She could feel the evil growing around Myrinas. The power tried to escape from her. She concentrated, pushing it beneath her. Across the chasm, she rode the fire. She could feel the energy draining from her as she landed on the other side. She slept for several more hours.

When she woke again, she realized her power had not fully returned. She must preserve it until the proper time came; the time that she once again faced the Dark Lord. And so she began to climb down. Just as Jason had walked, just as he had risen to the top with her, she began her decent into the unknown darkness below.

Sweat trickled down her forehead. Kristine could not remember feeling this much fear before in her life. She shuttered at the thought of the countless lives surrounded by a faceless evil. Someone needed to protect them. Tears welled up in her eyes. *How am I supposed to fight this?* She thought. *I just don't have enough power.*

She shut her eyes tightly to try to keep the tears from escaping. Kristine wanted to leave her fear behind. She forced her thoughts to happier times; simpler times.

Eight year old Jason and ten year old Kristine ran out of the village and into the hills. Jason laughed and teased Kristine as she tried to keep up. He was always faster than her. Kristine pulled and tugged at the grassy hill leading up to the Keash caves.

She always thought of them as their caves. It felt so magical to them. They would always come here to read stories together; this time it was Jason's turn to pick.

He stood and smiled cockily at her from the top of the hill.

"It isn't funny Jason!" Kristine grunted.

Just as she had almost reached the top she started to slip down. Jason reached down and pulled her, "You're never gonna learn, are ya Simmons? You can't take the same way I do or you'll slip to the bottom."

The cocky smile of the little boy grew wider. Kristine scowled. She hated when he did that but knew just the way to wipe the smug look off his face. She stood up next to him, leaned in, and kissed him.

Jason jumped, "Gross! Why do you always have to do that?" He started rubbing his cheek hard where she had kissed him.

"My hero," she said in an airy tone.

She had to turn away as she felt her face grow hot.

"Jason! Not again," she moaned when she saw the familiar picture of the Trojan horse. "You picked this one last *time."*

"So? It's my turn, and I pick this one. It's my favorite!"

"Fine, but you have to pick something else next time."

"We'll see."

The two sat side by side as Jason began to read aloud excitedly. Kristine's frustration with him subsided as he read on. His voice always calmed her down.

He read, "When night fell, they climbed silently out of the wooden horse."

Kristine snapped out of her day dream. *That's it,* she thought. She knew what she must do now. She ran disguises through her mind before settling in on the perfect one. It was simple and took very little power to keep herself disguised. Soon she resembled a frail old woman.

"Now, to slip into Myrinas and wait for the opportune moment," she whispered to herself.

11

Trek to Hamberidge

Rioridan and Arilie walked far behind Raza, whispering softly to one another, and eyeing him with distrust. The Raltiiri was a strange creature to them. It seemed evil, too, that he was the only one of his kind.

It was nothing new to Raza to have others speak ill of him, or to show him so much distrust. It was true that after his mother passed he remained the only of his kind. He could never explain from where he had come; his mother never told him. This past shrouded in mystery and the deep red of his fur led most to conclude he must be a demon.

Before he could remember, Raza had been taken into slavery with his mother by the Scythians when their race dominated following The War of the races. She was made to cook and care for the royalty. When he became old enough, he was made to carry weapons for the Trodaire, arena fighters, and remove dead bodies from the arena.

After some time of watching, Raza learned to fight. With his great agility, Raza was soon used as a training dummy for the Scythian warriors. After sixty years in slavery, he adapted to the language; though he spoke rarely, and even then, only to prisoners.

His mother made him swear he would get out and make a life for himself. He did not deserve the life of a slave. It was all too easy for him to escape. The Scythians had foolishly come to trust Raza, and even respect him for his exceptional ability to fight; not even the most skilled of the Trodaire could touch him. While training in the pits had commenced, no had one bothered to close the gates. Once his chains were removed, Raza tripped those training with him and broke through the gate before it could be closed. Dozens of guards attempted to stop him, but all quickly ended up on the ground.

He disarmed two more guards and stole one of their cloaks, then ran far from the mountain fortress of Shirauk. Each attempt to stop the Raltiiri fell short. Even with the superior riding skills the Scythians had, they could not match Raza's greater speed and agility. He went deep into the forest and came across a scouting party of Dwarves. Raza kept himself well concealed underneath the Scythian cloak until he was brought before Grodan Hamber. He shared with Grodan his tales of slavery among the Scythians. Raza was welcomed as a great friend and ally of the Dwarves. He trained them for the next year until they invaded Shirauk in an attempt to eradicate the evil that plagued the many lands.

The campaign was nearly a complete success. Few of the Dwarves fell under the Scythian blades. Raza went for his mother and found her, a knife held to her throat. The Scythian slit her throat before Raza's eyes. A handful of Scythians escaped in the confusion and despair. The Raltiiri laid his mother in the catacombs of Hamberidge at the request of the king. He swore a silent oath of vengeance upon the Scythians that remained.

It was this oath that drove him to continue on. Chance had led him to Tanas and had now brought him to the war that would give him ample opportunity to reach his goal at last. Once he had fulfilled his promise, he would try to find his people; if his people remained.

After the several days' walk, it was very simple for

Raza to locate the entrance to Hindling. The three travelers entered, lit a torch, and descended beneath the forest. Hindling was dark. The coals remaining in the braziers sat cold. No one answered their calls that echoed through the darkness; no life remained.

"Where would they have gone?" Rioridan asked

Raza did not need to think about it, "Home."

"Why would they do that? Wasn't their home overrun by Ogres?"

"Yes, but the Dwarves have been divided for far too long. They wished for their race to be reunited. Hamberidge is where they call home, and without that, they will always feel divided. Only Dorian saw this as a fool's errand." Raza sank to the ground. "I suggest you sleep. We will leave in a few hours. There is no telling how far ahead of us they are. If we are to catch them, we will need to move quickly. If we don't, they are doomed."

Both Elves obeyed unquestioningly; their hesitation remained buried deep in their minds. All three travelers dropped quickly off to sleep; Raza did not sleep deeply. Uneasiness grew in his heart. Each second that passed by was time Raza felt could be used searching for the Dwarves.

His heart beat with anxiety for his friends.

Hours still remained before sunrise when Raza roused the sleeping Elves, "Time to go."

This became the pattern over the next several weeks. The trail the Dwarves took remained difficult for Raza to find. The relationship between the Raltiiri and the Elves did not improve either. Raza grew more impatient and irritated with Rioridan and Arilie, as he had to stop often and wait for them to catch up, or back track so they did not lose him when he would find strong evidence of the Dwarves passing.

Not until three months had passed by did Raza finally find something. Black smoke rose in front of the setting sun. Cautiously Raza climbed over the next ridge. What dread he was already feeling only multiplied when the sight of flames hit his eyes. The scent was clearly the Dwarves.

A dozen Orcs stood watching the Dwarven settlement burn while laughing. The hair on Raza's body stood on end. Anger flowed through his veins. Were it not for his years of experience, Raza would have attacked immediately. Instead, he began to survey the area for any signs of life. The two Elves ran up behind Raza, panting. Due to their exhaustion, they were unable to take the same care as the Raltiiri. Raza glared angrily at them for breaking through the brush more noisily than they had intended.

When Raza turned back, three of the Orcs were missing.

"Look's like we have guests, boys!" A gruff voice came from behind them. The Orcs that had disappeared stood aiming crossbows at Raza and the two Elves.

"Throw your weapons over here," the biggest and ugliest of the three commanded. He was clearly in charge. Sharp yellow teeth showed through the gross smile on his face. Swords, daggers, and a hunting bow were thrown at the Orcs' feet. The smaller two Orcs gathered the weapons, then the leader barked, "You're coming with us."

With arrow tips in their backs, the three companions were led to the Orcs' camp outside the Dwarven settlement. The dozen they had seen by the settlement were only half of what was actually there. Twenty-one other Orcs sat around fires eating meat and drinking ale. They barely took notice of the return of their leader with prisoners.

Raza, Arilie, and Rioridan were led to the rear of the

camp where a large tent stood. Their hands and legs were tightly bound before they were thrown inside. The two Orcs that had taken their weapons stood guard outside the tent.

Inside was dark and smelled strongly of mold and feces. When Raza's eyes adjusted, he noticed someone sleeping in the far corner of the tent. A Dwarf, bound and naked, curled in a ball and facing away from them. Fresh cuts and bruises covered the body of the Dwarf. His breathing was shallow and mixed with coughs. Occasionally his body would shiver. The cool air of fall was setting in. This Dwarf's scent filled Raza's nostrils. Something familiar lay buried beneath the smell of blood, sweat and waste.

The Dwarf stirred, then, realizing he wasn't alone cowered further into his corner of the tent.

"Dorian?!" Raza looked at his friend who was definitely much frailer than the last time they has seen one another.

The prince managed a weak smile, "You never were great at rescues, my friend. Welcome to Brodaun."

Over the next several hours Dorian Hamber explained to Raza and the Elves about the journey to

Brodaun. How they had just managed to get the last of the settlers out before the Orcs attacked. They fought off as many as they could. Dorian stayed behind with a small battalion to hold them off, but was captured.

"And that was about two weeks ago. These Orcs wait for the rest of the warriors to return. It gives me some hope that my people have gotten safely to Fordring, and the Orcs were unable to catch them," Dorian concluded.

"We can only hope," Raza tried to mask the worry in his voice.

"So what do we do now?" Arilie asked hopelessly.

"Simple," Raza looked at Dorian, "We wait for nightfall, then leave."

Dorian smiled weakly at his friend. Arilie and Rioridan watched as Raza stretched his claws.

It was hard to tell when the sun fell inside the already dark tent. Raza listened carefully for the guard change outside before moving. As quietly as possible, he wormed his way next to Dorian, and carefully began cutting Dorian's ropes. Raza's sharp claws made quick work of the rope, and Dorian's bonds fell to the ground. In turn, Dorian untied Raza's hands from behind his back. All four were free within a few short minutes.

Raza stalked carefully to the closed flaps of the tent and listened for movement from the two Orcs standing guard. As expected, their breathing was shallow. Both were heavily asleep, and probably drunk. He slipped quietly outside while the others waited. Going left first, Raza's sharp claws cut through the flesh of the orc's throat while one hand covered the orc's mouth to muffle any sound. The dark blood oozed from the wound while the Orc looked up in horror at the burning eyes of Raza. In seconds, the Orc lay still.

Raza's ears perked as the second Orc, now behind him, began to stir. In one fluid motion Raza drew the sword of the fallen Orc and cut off the head of the other before a sound of alarm could be made. He pulled back the tent flap and beckoned his friend and Elvish companions to follow. Rioridan had removed his cloak and given it to the naked Dwarf. The two swords from the Orcs were handed to the Elves. Raza began moving stealthily toward the Orc camp.

"Where are you going?" Arilie whispered.

"To get my swords back from this scum," Raza

whispered back.

Dorian was quickly at his side, "Good, then I am going to get my armor back."

The Elves sighed in unison and followed.

It didn't take long to find the commander's tent among the others. It seemed the two Orcs Raza had killed were meant as charges over the sleeping camp. The four entered the tent. Embers glowed at the foot of the commander's bed. Raza spotted his swords hanging next to the Dwarf's armor and ax. Raza stepped to grab his weapons, Dorian following to get his armor. As the Raltiiri reached out, the Orc opened his eyes.

"The prisoners esca-," his call was cut short as the blade Arilie carried was buried in the Orc's chest.

"Well, this should be interesting," Dorian said aloud as he quickly pulled on his clothing and armor then tossed Rioridan's cloak back to him.

They rushed outside, weapons drawn, to find the camp fully awake and standing around the tent. Twenty-one Orcs surrounded them, armed with swords and axes. Raza leapt in the air, drawing his swords. The Orcs stood, stunned by the Raltiiri above them. In one swift motion, Raza grabbed a dagger with his tail and whipped it at an Orc. The blade buried in the Orc's neck, killing him. The Raltiiri landed between two others, and cut off their heads.

Dorian, Rioridan, and Arilie took their cue from the distraction. Left and right, Orcs fell to the ground until only one remained. Seeing the flawless fall of his comrades, he turned to run. Seeing the attempt, Dorian threw his ax at the fleeing Orc. He fell face first to the ground with the ax deep in his back.

The Dwarf walked over and ripped the ax out of the Orc, "There is no time to waste. We move on to Fordring."

The spirit of the Elves momentarily lifted at the thought of Dorian leading the way. They thought it would be much easier to follow a dwarf. After only three days they learned the Dwarf's drive and determination easily matched that of Raza. The exhausting trip from Brodaun to Fordring was taken off the trails to avoid detection and being followed.

After four weeks the walls of Fordring broke into view. Smoke rising hastened the travelers, giving them hope.

Atop a plateau far to the south, the white walls gleamed in the early morning sun. Except the black smoke burning, the entire city was white, blending evenly with the limestone of the plateau. Cautiously, the Elves followed Raza and Dorian into the open gates of Fordring.

"Relax," Raza said calmly, "the city is empty."

In the center of the city, a fire pit smoked quietly.

Dorian approached solemnly, "This fire burned out last night. Chances are they left a day or two ago."

"They're gone?!" Arilie asked a little angrier than intended, "What do we do now?"

Dorian turned from the fire and faced north, "There is only one place left for the Dwarves to go; back home to Hamberidge."

Plans were made. Since the Dwarves were only a couple days ahead, they would travel directly north in hopes to overcome them and stop them from walking into the heart of the Ogre population. To the distaste of Arilie and Rioridan, the journey would be fast paced with very few, short stops. Worst for the Elves, they were leaving immediately.

A day into the journey, an early snow storm blew in on the autumn wind, blanketing the ground. Raza removed his cloak and handed it silently to Arilie, who was shivering uncontrollably. She looked confusedly at the Raltiiri and mouthed a thank you before pulling the warm wool tunic over her head.

Weeks passed, and no sign of the other Dwarves could be found. Raza back tracked while the other three moved on, and still found nothing. As early winter approached, Dorian assured them Hamberidge was only two days' journey north, and if they found nothing, they would wait.

Heavy snow storms slowed them down. After three days the mountains broke way. A blanket of white was seen overlooking the valley that held Hamberidge. No life could be detected below. They crept cautiously closer, using the trees and banks of snow as cover. It was clear that Hamberidge had been abandoned by the Ogres, and it appeared to be void of dwarves as well. Dorian walked toward the home he had once known, confused at the absence of life. His legs dragged through the deep snow. His foot caught something, and he fell face first into the snow. Raza ran forward to aid his friend, but stopped just feet away at the sight of what Dorian had tripped on.

The fears Raza had felt rushed back into him instantly when he saw the uncovered body of a dead Dwarf. His eyes wide with horror, he began scanning around. It became suddenly apparent to him; all the bodies buried almost entirely by the snow.

"They are all dead," Raza hissed. Dorian stood and looked around with tears forming in his eyes. His people had come seeking to retake their home from the Ogres only to be slaughtered.

"Start searching the bodies," Dorian commanded, "See if any are still alive. I'm going inside to see if anyone still remains. Perhaps my father is still here."

Dorian stumbled inside the giant doors of Hamberidge while the other three dug through the snow, checking for survivors.

After several hours of searching dead bodies Arilie called out, "Over here, I've found someone that is alive."

Dorian, Raza and Rioridan rushed over to the Elf girl.

Dorian knelt next to the dying Dwarf, "Can you tell

us what happened here?"

"Water," the Dwarf pleaded quietly.

Arilie poured some water in the Dwarf's mouth.

He then spoke, "We came, all of us. We thought maybe, with time, we might have grown strong enough to take our home back. Three of us stayed behind at Fordring for a week waiting for you to arrive. When you didn't come, we left. As soon as we got here, everyone was already dead. We were attacked as the last of the Ogres marched out of here. I was thrown from the ridge; the other two were pulled apart."

He began to cough up blood violently. Arilie took his hand. The coughing stopped and the Dwarf was barely breathing.

"Is there anything else you can remember?" Dorian asked, barely processing the death of so many, "Please."

"Myr-i-nas," the Dwarfs chest fell but did not rise again.

"No! Damned Ogres!" Dorian's scream echoed for several seconds before he broke down, weeping for the annihilation of his entire race. "I'll kill every last one of them," he tried to yell through his sobs.

Raza knelt down and embraced his friend, who cried into the Raltiiri's chest.

Arilie and Rioridan gathered as much dry wood as they could find and built a fire while Raza consoled his dearest friend. The next morning, all four went to work, burying as many of the dead as they were able to find in the deep snow. The last to be buried was Grodan Hamber, king of the Dwarves. Dorian was left alone to mourn for his father, whom he had buried next to his mother.

Finally, Dorian walked to his companions, showing much more composure than they expected, "We move on to Myrinas as was planned. Perhaps we can aid a little, if nothing else."

As they left the valley, Dorian turned and looked back one last time on the home he would never return to.

12

Eulogy

The Prophet arrived several days after riding out from the Elven city Midlothian. He rode straight through the gates of Myrinas and on to the temple without stopping. The Elders were just leaving as Tanas arrived; their spirits lifted at the sight of Tanas.

"We are so pleased to see you have returned, Prophet." Ardel approached him, "You just missed your father. He said he had urgent preparations for the coming war."

A stable boy took the reins of the horse after Tanas dismounted. Tanas hastily climbed the stairs and stopped at the doors. Without turning he said, "Inform me the moment he returns. Disturb me for nothing else." The council nodded in agreement to this request.

Several weeks after Tanas's arrival, an attempt was made to contact the Prophet when a boy carried the unconscious Oracle to the city gates. He waved the messenger away without looking up from the book he read or hearing a word that was said.

Days later, an old hag hobbled from the shadows of a nearby alley and approached the temple. She was dressed in tattered brown robes and supported by a wooden cane that looked as if it had been picked straight off the forest floor.

Ardel stopped her just before she reached the stairs, "I am sorry, but the Prophet will see no one at this time."

Her emerald eyes sparkled as she pleaded, "Please, its imperative I speak with him."

"I am afraid," Ardel seemed pained this time by his answer, "Tanas will see no one until his father returns."

The pleading in the old woman's eyes changed to sorrow as she hobbled away, perhaps more agilely than and old woman should. *By then it will be too late,* she thought as she entered the alley she had come from. Ardel felt compelled to ask the woman her name but when he reached the alley way she had vanished. From a roof top across from the temple the woman watched as guards were posted outside and instructed to not let the hag anywhere near the temple.

For months the old woman watched the temple. At times she would attempt to enter, but she was chased off by the guards, though they could never seem to catch her, and she would mysteriously disappear after running around a corner. She located the window where she watched Tanas study scrolls and books that had been scattered through the Oracle's chamber. She knew he was searching for answers to the Dark Lord's being. Tanas seemed determined to find a way to stop him.

The hag knew the histories revealed nothing of the Dark Lord. The old wars and alliances held no keys. The writings of past prophets said nothing of the Dark Lord. Soon, books were stacked on the floor, and scrolls left rolled out on the bed. The shelves were empty, and he appeared to have discovered nothing. Only she had the knowledge that Tanas was seeking, but she had not yet found a way into the temple that was not guarded.

"Come on Tanas," she whispered, "You must know that nothing is there. You have to listen to what is in your heart."

The Prophet looked up from the writings, as if he had heard something. Then, deciding it was nothing shook it off as just a trick of his mind from lack of sleep. She watched from her perch late into the night. Below, the guards changed shifts. Tanas had fallen asleep; only a single candle burned in the chamber of the Oracle. The old hag fought off sleep as the moon reached the center of the sky. Just before her eyelids closed, a shout roused her back to consciousness. It took several times before she made out what was being said.

"He's here! He's here! Just as he promised, Silamond has returned to us!"

The call continued as Silamond came into view. His black robes flowed around his body as he walked swiftly to the temple. In the sky to the south dark storm clouds were swiftly approaching, as if they followed Silamond to the city. The doors seemed to open of their own accord, and Silamond continued into the temple. Ardel approached the temple, but the doors slammed shut before he reached the stairs. Despite the late hour, much of the city had awakened and gathered around the temple. They waited anxiously for Tanas and Silamond to emerge.

Hidden among the roof tops, the old woman felt

tense. Things were falling apart quickly inside Myrinas. The temperature was dropping at an unnatural rate. She made her way back to the open window. Tanas had been awakened by his father's arrival. The small flame on the candle flickered out, so all the woman could make out were the shadows of the two men that were very similar. She tried to see through the darkness, but once they spoke, she was even more confused; the voices sounded like the same man.

"How dare you return here and defile these people!" one said.

"It was my duty to return here," said the other, "They need protection. They need a ruler."

"And you feel like you are the best fit? HA!"

"Better than you ever could be. I've gone further than any other prophet could dream. I have gained more power than any other soul that has stepped foot inside these walls."

"Your gain came at the cost of Leara!"

"How dare you speak *her* name in my presence," the second shadow lifted his arm and struck the other in the face.

"Does it pain you to hear her name? It is your fault she is dead after all," A flash of blue light broke from the first man, throwing the other hard against the wall.

The second started laughing. The dark laughter caused an icy chill to creep down the old woman's spine.

He stood and approached the first slowly, "Her death was a mistake. Yours will, unfortunately, be necessary."

The old woman gasped when she noticed the first man pull something from his cloak; it appeared to be a dagger. The second continued his slow approach.

The first spoke, "It won't be my blood spilled tonight, it will be yours."

He lunged at the second man, who side stepped and hit the first down to the ground. The second man extended his arm, and the first was raised into the air. He began to scream in pain as the second approached him. The dagger was pulled from the first man's hand.

The second spoke, "I never wanted it to be this way. I loved you both dearly, and only wanted you to rule by my side. As with Leara, I am sorry to see you go."

The first man struggled to move, but to no avail, "No…"

His scream was cut short as the second man buried the dagger into the first man's chest. He was dropped to the floor. The lights in the temple burst to life as the second man fled the room. The woman made her way back to the front of the temple just in time to see the doors burst open. Silamond emerged, panting heavily.

A false hint of grief was in his voice, "My son tried to kill me. He… he is dead."

Heaviness filled the air such as this generation had never known. Though they felt the Oracle still lived, she still had not returned to them with the boy that had carried her up the Misty Mountain. This night's events, however, were a tragedy none had thought they would see. The great prophet Tanas had fallen.

The black clouds continued roll in until the sky was engulfed in darkness. Cold drops of rain fell from the sky. This was always the case with the death of a prophet. The planet wept for her fallen; rain fell for three days, then cleared. The body would be placed at the center of the city, and the people would gather. The Oracle would offer a eulogy before the body was then burned, and the prophet became a part of the planet.

This time, that was not the case. After a week the rains still fell and grew steadily colder. With the Oracle not returning, it was decided they could not wait any longer. Silamond asked for the body to be prepared. He would eulogize his son. He would offer Tanas to Myriad.

The Prophet's body was brought to the center of the city. Every citizen of Myrinas was present, heads bowed and thick wool cloaks protecting them from the icy rain. Silamond climbed the platform erected for the occasion. His face was hidden by the black cowl covering his head. The noise of the storm dissipated as the heavy rain turned to snow and began blanketing everything in icy white. The old woman continued to watch the city from the rooftops. The air grew colder as the voice of the Silamond carried to every ear.

"There could have been no Prophet greater to lead this people than my son. His visions and prophecies were always precise. He was never wrong of forthcoming events. His heart was always open for this city. He knew and loved each of you individually. The knowledge he possessed surpassed nearly every prophet before him. I have never known of a more powerful protection than the one he provided."

Tears fell from every eye watching.

"Under the great care of Tanas, Myrinas had never known such great peace and protection in its lifetime."

A chill filled the air.

"Only he could foretell the future of Myrinas while the city remained in his charge. It was because of my son that evil feared this great city. It was a shame he fell to such great anger and jealousy that he would try to take my life. No parent wishes to see the end of their child, especially by their own hand."

Behind the gathering the city gates closed, though none took notice. A blanket of snow covered up the sound of footsteps around them. The old woman pulled her cloak tighter around her. She felt the encroaching evil - felt what was happening to her city.

"But with the fall of one leader, so must another rise, like a phoenix from the ashes."

Tanas body burst into bright blue flames. The crowd let out a gasp. Cold air radiated from the fire. Silamond's cowl fell behind him and a sinister smile stretched across his face. His entire being was shrouded by dark aura. The body of Tanas was completely engulfed as the flames grew higher. The entire city grew darker.

"The time has at long last come that I shall rule over this city. Now bow before the Dark Lord, Silamond!"

Silamond's hands rose above his head and the fire exploded skyward. Every man, woman and child felt the hand of the Dark Lord force them down to their knees then felt their heads forced downward. Fear overcame them. Above, the old woman wept in silence, unseen powerless to do anything. Her city had fallen to the rule of the Dark Lord. She had failed.

When the bowed heads were allowed to lift, screams of terror filled the square. Surrounding them stood thousands of heavily armed Ogres and Orcs. All the dark creatures saluted their master.

"With the death of my son," the pleasure went unmasked in Silamond's voice, "and the imminent return of the powerless Oracle Saedin," The crowd began to murmur, but fell silent again as Silamond raised his hand, "this world belongs to me! A new era has begun. All who join willingly will be greatly rewarded, while those who refuse…"

Silamond stopped talking when the scene before him caught his eye. What had before been deep blue flames had changed to a beam of bright white light. Warmth filled the people of Myrinas. The flames began to shrink down, but the light grew stronger. Where the Prophet's body had been, lay a glassy orb that emitted the light.

The orb rose slowly into the air. Every eye was locked to it. The light inside began to pulsate.

As it did, the voice of Tanas could be heard, "Fear not, children of Myrinas. My power has not diminished. This season of suffering will not last long. The one who will deliver you prepares, and will shortly arrive. The power of the Dark Lord will be vanquished."

Blue flames shot from Silamond's finger tips, "My power is endless!"

The orb absorbed the fire, "The Dark Lord will fall." With its last words, the orb flew up into the sky and out of sight.

*   *   *

Despair overcame the hearts of the people of Myrinas. They lived and worked as slaves under the controlling hand of Silamond. Day and night they were driven to serve him by making weapons and fortifying the city, cooking and caring for his army, while given little to eat for themselves. The despair was fueled by the constant cold and darkness. Sunlight never entered the city.

Rumors floated through the city that gave some hope. A mysterious old hag with emerald eyes was helping people flee. It seemed a possibility, since people began to vanish. Some speculated the Dark Lord was taking and punishing them for taking extra rations, or for not working hard enough. These rumors died once Silamond could be seen punishing his army for the unexplained disappearances.

For some, the mysterious old hag was all they needed to go on another day. Perhaps this was their deliverer.

13

Isles of the Dead

"…love you," Jason attempted to open his eyes, but closed them quickly while his eyes adjusted to the bright light.

"I love you too, Jason," came the soft sound of a woman's voice Jason did not recognize.

When he opened his eyes again, Jason was sure he had died. The sun shined brightly behind the figure of a woman that could be nothing other than an angel. Bright white wings were folded behind her. Her long blonde hair hung down in front of her as she knelt over Jason, smiling widely. Though her beautiful face was very young something deep inside Jason told him he knew this woman very well.

"Mom?"

The woman's smile broadened and seemed to make the sun glow brighter, "Yes, Jason, I am your mother."

Jason stood and looked down. He was dressed all in white. He lifted his shirt; no sign that a sword had gone through him remained. Finally, he scanned his surroundings. Hundreds of angels, men, women, and even children, watched the reunion of mother and son. They all stared at him with awe and respect, then in unison, knelt and bowed down to him.

"Why are they bowing," he turned back to his mother.

"Because you are the rightful heir to the throne of our people," Akarah was looking into Jason's eyes, "Because when the time comes, you will take up the throne and become Eraul."

Jason looked at her puzzled.

She clarified further, "King of Angels, Jason."

Jason looked over the crowed of Angels that stretched to the edge of the island. By all appearance the island was floating on a sea of clouds; in the distance, other smaller islands could be seen with people standing on them. It reminded Jason of pictures of the Alps he had seen where the peaks broke out above the clouds. Only the islands were covered in lush green grass and thousands of people.

"Is this heaven?" he asked.

Akarah laughed, "No, Jason. This is the Isles of the Dead."

"So I'm..." Jason choked on his words but was unable to finish.

A large man with blonde hair and deep blue eyes like Akarah came traipsing through the crowd.

"Get up. He's not Eraul yet," the brusque voice fit the man Jason thought looked like a king, "Go on, get out of here. We have work to do."

The titan of an Angel waved his hands. Like a flock of birds, the bowing Angels took flight and spread out to various islands surrounding what was clearly the largest. Jason, Akarah and what looked to be the largest of the Angels were left alone on the island.

"We should get started," the large man pulled two swords off his back and tossed one at Jason's feet, "Well, what are you waiting for? Pick it up."

Akarah looked sternly at the man, "What do you think you are doing?"

"A sword through the chest did not give him his wings. I am going to train the kid and force them out."

"There is more to it than that with him. He is holding on to too much. The necessity of his wings has not been enough. He has to let go of the things that are holding him back."

"And I intend to make that happen," the Angel spread his wings to their full span; each wing as nearly long as he was tall.

He raised the sword above his head with both hands and leapt into the air toward Jason. Jason stumbled backwards watching the sword coming down toward him. Before the large Angel came to the ground, Akarah stepped in the way and punched him in the stomach stopping his assault.

He let out a deep grunt and landed on the ground,

"Why did you get in the way?"

"This is not the way to do it, father!" Akarah seemed like a defiant toddler not getting her way. Jason thought by the difference in size it appeared very much that way. He watched them argue silently, seeing nothing more than his mother making large gestures and looking nervously back at him.

Finally their argument broke out of the seemingly silent bubble as the voice of the titan exploded through the air, "Your way is too slow and foolish. We will do it my way. There is little time left before all hope is lost, Akarah. You are my daughter, and here, you *will* listen to me."

"Fine," she conceded angrily and stomped off, and sitting hard on the ground.

Jason's eyes never left his mother. He felt a breeze move across his body from the left side. Something told him to duck and roll to his left. He got out of the way just in time. The blade broke apart the ground where Jason had been laying.

Aris had a look of surprise on his face when he saw Jason was already back on his feet, "I see you've had some training."

"Are you crazy?" Jason yelled, "You could have cut me in half!"

Jason had always been taller than most, but Aris easily towered over him. The sword came at Jason's head. He ducked and rolled out of the way; this time his hand connected with the hilt of a sword lying in the grass.

He was ready this time as Aris swung his sword again. The force caused Jason to lose his grip on the sword. It flew away from him, sticking in the ground well out of reach. Jason's body tingled as if warning him of the next attack, but he was confused. His senses could not tell him where to go. Aris's foot kicked hard into his grandson's stomach. Jason went up in the air and landed hard on his back twenty feet from where he had been standing.

Aris flew over to Jason, who groaned in pain. He lifted the sword over his head and brought it down hard again. Jason was unable to move. He closed his eyes and flinched. The sword stabbed hard into the ground. Jason felt the cold steel against his face.

Aris's voice sent warm spikes through Jason's body, "You let one ounce of fear in and your instincts lose focus. This is when your enemies finish you. Again."

Aris's large hand reached down and Jason was pulled up in a standing position once more. This time Jason felt more prepared as the sword was handed to him. He took a deep breath and focused on the training he'd had with Gaibian. He could feel the movement of the blades of grass around his feet. He concentrated harder and could soon feel the grass on the entire island. He would not be taken off guard again. Jason raised his sword and kept his eyes sharply focused on his grandfather. He blinked.

When Jason opened his eyes Aris was gone. An instant later Jason fell forward on the ground after Aris kicked him hard in the back of the head. Slowly he pushed himself up, coughing up blood.

Aris pulled Jason back to standing, and handing him the sword said, "Your enemies' attacks will never be the same. Again."

Over and over again Jason was knocked down, but by some miraculous force, the wounds would be healed and the only visible signs of training were bruises where the cuts had been. With each blow he took, Jason felt himself growing stronger and faster. Every time he lasted just a little longer against Aris's ruthless attacks. Time seemed to be lost in this place. There was no separation of one day to the next.

Outside the islands, the days and nights turned to weeks, the weeks to months. Soon the world was blanketed in fresh, white snow and ice surrounded the lakes and rivers. The isles themselves, however, remained as warm and green as late spring.

At last the time had come to move forward. Attack after attack was deflected by Jason.

Aris stopped, "Good, you've made excellent progress. Now that you know how to fight, you must learn to survive."

"Wait, what are you mean 'survive'?" Jason asked.

"You will not just be fighting an enemy that will attack you externally. The darkness will attack you from the inside."

Jason began feeling cold, "I still don't understa-" He started to choke before he could finish speaking.

Darkness covered his eyes. Jason fell to his knees. His hands dug into the dirt as he felt his entire body being crushed on all sides. Blood seeped from every pore of his body, soaking the ground beneath him.

"Do you understand yet, Jason?" Aris's voice seemed to be in Jason's mind, "This is the magnitude of pain that will come if you do not embrace who you are. You were born to become a guardian of light; as were all of us. The sins of our past must be atoned for."

Just as Jason felt the cold darkness would destroy him, the crushing ceased. He collapsed to the ground, panting heavily. A bucket of warm water was thrown on him, washing away the blood.

"Okay," Jason said as he rolled to his back. He struggled to keep his breathing even, as if he had just been choked, "I." -Cough- "Get." -Cough- "It." He steadied his breathing as best he could and sat up with difficulty, "What do I have to do?"

Akarah stepped toward Jason, giving her father a look of gratitude for doing what she could not.

"Now that you understand the pain you can feel for complete strangers," Aris faced Jason, "you can understand why you must remove yourself from them. Further, you must learn to let go of those you love."

Jason clenched his firsts to ensure he had mobility of his muscles. Every inch of him screamed with pain. With each breath, his lungs pushed against his ribs. He was sure several were broken.

Through great struggle and concentration, Jason had steadied himself, "I can do this without letting her go." -Jason stood up hiding the pain- "She's the only reason I'm even here." He faced Aris, forcing strength into his eyes. Without breaking his gaze, he bent down and picked up the discarded sword. "Again."

The blackness was more intense than before. Jason felt as if his entire body was made of ice. The air was expelled from his lungs, and he lost consciousness. In the darkness, the faces of the couple Jason had recognized as parents floated before him. They smiled at him. He attempted to reach out to them, but his body was paralyzed. Slowly, they faded away. Their faces became completely washed out by a bright, white light. When Jason's vision cleared, Akarah's face hovered above him. His body felt warm.

"Am I dead?" he asked weakly.

Akarah laughed, "You sure like to ask that a lot."

"Why do you keep avoiding the question?" he asked.

"It is irrelevant," she avoided Jason's eyes.

"Irrelevant?" Jason shot up, "Did I die or not?!"

Hot water broke out around him. He stopped; it looked to him like he had been soaking in a hot spring. Steam rose up from the stirred waters.

Akarah smiled at her son, "It would be difficult for you to understand."

Jason sighed and sunk back into the warm pool. He stared up at the cloudless blue sky.

His mother's face appeared above his, "Jason, it is difficult for us to really know because your soul never left your body. When you were carried you over the edge of the cliff, I caught you and flew you back here. Your heart had stopped and you weren't breathing. The water that comes from the fountain in Ojai has remarkable healing abilities. Some of the water had pooled inside you. The cut remained open, but the water had started to mend your body. The reaction of the water with our blood, the blood of Angel, was something we have never witnessed. It was remarkable watching the way your body healed from the inside out then sealed the hole flawlessly. It was then that your heart started beating and you opened your eyes.

"We still cannot figure out is why your wings have yet to appear. Mine came as a reflex to protect me. I assumed yours would do the same. It's very important that you have them. Our wings are a part of us- an extension of our being. They act as a shield to protect us. They increase our power and our talents exponentially. There is no magic that can penetrate them. No force that can break them. Without them, you will never be able to defeat Silamond. Even though you are an Angel, when you are in your human state, you are nearly as vulnerable as a human. That's why you are being pushed so hard. You need to reach a breaking point where the only other option to survive is your wings. But I am starting to wonder if you will reach that point," Akarah sighed and looked at her father, who had been watching and listening intently. Without looking at Jason, she finished, "You have to want it, Jason."

Aris nodded in approval, "It is time he returned. We can do nothing more for him here."

Jason stood and let the water fall from him,

"Again."

Aris smiled, "Your determination amazes even me. Put this on." Aris stepped aside revealing magnificent silver plate armor. Jason put it on; it was as light as a feather and was just as quiet. He could move around as easily as if he was only wearing the clothing beneath.

His confidence rose, and a question fell from his mouth he had never imagined, "How long have I been here?"

A tense silence lingered heavy in the air.

Akarah looked awkwardly to her father, and then back to Jason, "You have been here for a year, son."

Jason looked back and forth from Akarah to Aris. The truth sunk in. Jason turned and walked away from his mother and grandfather.

Akarah followed after Jason, "Where are you going?"

"I'm getting off of this stupid island," Jason yelled behind him, "We're wasting time. Kristine's in trouble and she needs me."

Jason started into a run then jumped out over the Seas of the Damned in a dive. Akarah grabbed his ankle, pulling him back. He landed hard on his stomach letting out a grunt.

"Listen to me," she said, with every sternness of a mother, "if you enter the water of the Seas of the Damned you will do more damage than you can possibly imagine. I will take you back, but I can only go as far as the shore. From there, you're on your own."

"Fine, just get me off of here," Jason stood and faced his mother.

Aris approached Jason, "Take my sword with you. If you have learned anything, it will help you reach your goal."

For the first time since arriving, Jason saw the loving gentleness in his grandfather's eyes. He wrapped his arms around Aris and felt the Angel's powerful arms wrap around him. Jason felt warm as the power of Aris consumed his body.

"The mantle of Light I hold is now yours, you have earned it. Goodbye, my grandson."

The two separated from the embrace and turned away from each other. Akarah took Jason under his arms, spread her wings, and flew up into the air and over the Seas of the Damned.

Jason looked down. It seemed as if they were soaring over a sea of white clouds; the same sea of clouds surrounding the isles. He peered deeper and began to feel very cold. Something wasn't right. The clouds were changing to gray as lightning streaked across the surface. The clouds began to part along the path they were flying. Jason knew he should turn away, but could not bring himself to do it.

"Come to us Jason," an icy voice pierced to his heart, "help us Jason."

The sensation of flying completely left Jason. He now felt like he was slowly falling. The break in the clouds seemed to be getting bigger. It took several seconds for Jason to realize it wasn't getting bigger, he was getting closer. He *was* falling!

"Yes Jason, that's right. Come to us. Free us!" The voice felt like a vice on Jason's lungs.

He struggled to breath. His arms and legs began

flailing. The closer he got, the colder he felt. Just inches from reaching the surface Jason stopped and felt his frozen body rising back in the air. When feeling returned to him, he felt the warmth of his mother; her arms wrapped tight around his waist. Jason continued to shiver, not from the cold, but from the fear.

"I've got you son," Akarah whispered into Jason's ear, "You must never touch this water. There is no returning from the Seas of the Damned."

Akarah let Jason down just beyond the water's edge, "Remember, Jason, never touch this water. The repercussions would be irreversible."

14

The War Begins

For the fifth consecutive night Jerech awoke from his sleep in a cold sweat. His breathing was heavy as the last thing he saw in the Orbs of Ojai burned fresh in his mind.

The battle has momentarily stopped. Jerech stands at the head of the army. A light breaks through the dark clouds, completely surrounding Jerech. Incomprehensible mumblings are heard from both armies. Jerech's body jerks as an arrow strikes his heart. He falls dead. Seconds later he watches from above as his army is annihilated by Orc armies flooding over them from the North, and a second army flanking them from the South preventing an escape.

It was always the same dream. It was what the Orbs had shown Jerech; his end and the end of Elves and Men.

Soreilia slipped silently through the door, carrying a tray with two cups and a pot of tea. She had grown used to the consistency of the nightmares and begun showing up as Jerech would wake, "Hot tea, my Lord?"

Jerech took the cup, "Thank you Soreilia."

The king was grateful to have her present. He had something he had meant to discuss with her and it seemed there wasn't much time to do it; the army would be preparing to leave in a few hours and Jerech would not be returning.

"Soreilia, I need you to know that I love you very much, and must request you remain here in Midlothian. My sons are gone. You are like a daughter to me, and you know our people better than any," Soreilia opened her mouth to speak, but Jerech stopped her, "Please let me finish; this is already difficult enough for me. Before Gaibian took the orbs, I saw something I have feared would come. We go to war, but this battle will be my last. I will not be returning."

Soreilia's eyes were filled with tears, "Then don't go! Since my mother died, you are all I have. If you don't go, you won't die."

"I wish it were that simple," Jerech took Soreilia's

hand, "If I do not go, there will be no success. Our people will be destroyed. It is my duty to go. It is my destiny to have my life come to an end here. I have failed as a king, and as a father. I allowed my only sons to come to a complete destruction. I used the orbs to rule Midlothian in every aspect. None of what we have…"

"Stop it," Soreilia stood and screamed at Jerech through her tears, "Stop talking like this! It is not your fault. You can change it. You can make it better."

"I wish I could, but it is too late. It is out of my hands."

"No, I won't let this happen! I'll find a way to stop it," Soreilia ran from the room. Jerech tried to follow, but when he reached the door, she was already gone.

"I am sorry, my daughter," for so many years Jerech had wanted to say those words; to tell her *he* was her real father.

*   *   *

Jason stood at the edge of the black water, watching as his mother flew over the Seas of the Damned and out of sight.

"I will save her. And I won't let you down," Jason whispered toward Akarah. A haze settled along the ground so thick Jason was certain he could feel it. The sludgy black water seemed to be creeping up the shore toward Jason. He stepped back. It took the form of hands, clawing for Jason, trying to drag him toward the water.

The familiar cold whisper entered his mind again, "Come Jason. I will give you the power to stop your enemies and free the ones you love. I can help you."

The wind picked up at Jason's back and began to push him toward the grasping hands as the voice repeated the words inside him. He was nearly within reach when he began to fight back. A shudder went through is body. *Never touch the waters*, his mother's voice whispered to his heart. He had nearly done the first thing he was told not to. Jason dug his heels into the sandy beach to fight against the wind. Slowly, he was able to inch further away from the water. The hands retracted back to the sea.

A large bubble formed in the water and molded itself into a giant head. "You will pay for your insolence son of Angels," The same cold voice that had been only a whisper before now boomed loudly, "I, Draedin, will personally see to your destruction, and make sure that you never succeed in saving your loved ones. The day will come when you will have to face me, Jason England, and that will be the day you die!"

The head vanished, and the water lay still.

Jason did not this allow his resolve to become shaken. He turned and began walking north. He trekked through worn and overgrown paths. Rain clouds hung low, blocking out the sun. Jason was grateful for this, since it kept the air cool. It wasn't until nightfall that the rain came. Heavy drops of water fell from the sky, soaking Jason through the armor. He found a hollowed out tree that gave him cover from the harsh rain, allowing him a few hours sleep.

He woke as the sun would have broken over the horizon. The night's rain had ceased, but the clouds remained. Jason kept moving in hopes that he could to keep warm. The damp clothing stuck his body and was very uncomfortable under the metal armor. The battered road was now thick with mud making the journey more difficult. Meals consisting of wild berries, nuts and roots sustained him throughout the day. As night fell, so did the rain.

This pattern continued for several days. Cold, cloudy days growing more difficult with each step taken followed by rainy nights where shelter was hard to come by. Little food to strengthen Jason as thoughts of doubt slowly filled his mind. On the fifth day, the broken pathway Jason had been following came to a sudden end. A rustling in the trees set his instincts on fire. He unsheathed the sword strapped to his back. Slowly he stepped from the pathway into the darkened trees. His heart pounded in his chest. As quietly as possible, Jason crept toward the rustling. He was nearly there. He pressed his back against a tree; the sound was coming from the other side.

Jason jumped around to the opposite side letting out an intimidating yell. What he saw made him fall to his knees in a fit of laughter.

"All that for a rabbit," he said embarrassed. In front of him a brown rabbit stood frozen. It was wrapped tightly in vines along the base of the tree. Its struggle to free itself had only caused the rabbit to become more entangled. Jason reached out slowly and the rabbit began to struggle harder.

Jason stopped, "No, shhhh. I'm not going to hurt you."

The rabbit stopped struggling and stared blinkingly at Jason's kind eyes as if understanding him. Jason broke apart the vines until the rabbit was free. He stood and watched as it raced away into the thick trees before he continued north again.

The sound of thunder echoed through the trees. Jason knew that was his cue to find shelter; night was coming again. For the first time in days, Jason felt fortunate; he found a cave deep enough to shelter him from the rain and build a small fire. He gathered up as much dry wood as possible, started a fire, and then drifted quickly off to sleep. When the rain stopped falling, Jason woke. He kicked the dry dirt from the cave over the glowing embers of his fire. As he stepped out of the cave, he felt a thick, foreboding darkness creeping through the forest. Something was near….something large - something evil.

In what felt like only minutes, Jason reached a break in the trees. A large clearing opened up and held the answer to what Jason had felt.

The army stood in perfect unison; north of the clearing. Thousands of highly trained Orcish warriors perfectly seasoned and bred for a single battle. Formations were being made without a single word being spoken.

Plans had been drawn out well in advance. The archers lined up just behind the foot soldiers. All awaited the order from the hooded figure mounted on a dark horse before them. The horse let out a long, low growl. Fiery steam from the horse's nostrils could be seen in the early morning cold.

The grass was still wet from the previous nights' rain. Large puddles flooded the field, but did not deter a single wretched soul. The Dark Lord's orders were final, and nothing would stop this army from wiping out the last of the resistance between here and Myrinas, which had already been taken by the Dark Lord.

A lone figure standing at the southern end of the clearing, Jason was exhausted from traveling. He had gotten very little rest for days. The armor was heavy on the shoulders and the damp clothing cold on his worn body. The sword strapped to his back felt heavier than it should. Breathing slowly, he did all in his power to keep from collapsing to the ground.

The figure on the horse turned, and for the first time, noticed Jason standing at the opposite end of the clearing. His hood fell behind his head, revealing an extremely ugly and disfigured Orc. Scars covered his face. Half the Orc's nose was missing, as well as an ear. He signaled to one of the archers standing nearby. One by one the Orcs began to turn until they were all facing Jason. Several laughed.

A single arrow left the bow of the archer hat had been alerted by his commander. Jason stood unmovable, watching the arrow come toward him. It felt as if time had slowed as he watched the arrow pierce his armor just above his left breast. It went through his body until the point of the arrow was protruding out the back of his armor. He looked at the arrow stuck in him. Hot pain filled his chest and back. No sound came as he stood in awe of this foreign pain to his body. Before he could react, a second arrow hit the right side of his body stopping deep in his abdomen. The force spun him around and he fell to his knees leaving his back exposed to the enemy.

Jason lifted his head with much difficulty. A dark-haired transparent figure stood before him. Her arms were folded, a look of anger and disappointment on her face.

"Get up Jason, I need your help. Don't leave me alone. It's so cold. I'm afraid. I know you can save me. Please don't give up."

He reached up to her, but before he could touch her, the figure changed.

"Son, there may be no hope left for the people of this world."

Jason's mother with the same expression that had been on Kristine's face.

"Jason," Akarah stepped toward her wounded son, "Don't do this."

"Please," Akarah said, "It's not worth your life; I don't want to lose you again."

As Akarah approached, the figure changed again. The third figure lowered down do one knee in front of Jason.

"You have traveled a long way, young prince," Aris's said, "You have a great choice before you that only you can make." Aris held out his left hand to Jason, "You can go back to the life you knew before coming to this world. This will all have been just a crazy dream, and you can continue on with your old life as if nothing happened. The other option," he put out his right hand, "you can continue on this fool's errand which, ultimately, leads to your death. Jason, you have no destiny. You make your choices; your life is your own to decide. No one can tell you how it must be lived. Take my hand to be free of this or continue down the path you've started. I offer only one warning, certain death lies behind you."

Jason struggled to keep his head up to look at the figure before him. His eyes went from the arrow in his chest up to meet the eyes of his grandfather.

"You have one thing right," Jason began to breath heavily.

He reached behind and broke the tip off the tip of the arrow embedded in his chest. Gritting his teeth, he pulled the arrow out and tossed it to the side.

"My life is my own" he said as he stood up, never taking his eyes off the image of Aris.

Without hesitation, Jason grabbed the shaft of the arrow in his stomach and pulled it out. Blood fell slowly from the open wounds, staining the ground beneath him.

The figure of Aris became distorted and changed to a figure in a dark hood. Shiny black horns rounded upward out of the hood; red, fiery eyes burned from within. A black, clawed finger pointed at Jason from the dark cloak. "Your day will come, Prince," spat the same cold voice Jason remembered from the Seas of the Damned.

"My servant has claimed Myrinas and soon, all of Myriad will be mine. It will not be long before I am free of this wretched prison and see to your destruction. The world you come from will burn, and so will this one."

"No Draedin. As long as there is a breath in my body, Myriad will never be yours," Jason held the gaze of the demonic apparition. "As for Earth, it is far from being in your hands," Jason turned, his eyes burned into the army across from him, "and I'll be damned if I let your evil poison it!" His voice carried across to the ears of the Orcs, and they all burst into loud, mocking laughter.

The archer reloaded his bow and shot an arrow, followed quickly by another. Each buried themselves into Jason's legs, one after the other. He collapsed once more to the ground. When Jason tried to stand again, a blue jay landed in front of him. He eyed the bird curiously. *Why would a bird willingly land next to me* especially *when so much danger is here?*

It looked up at him as if it *knew* him. In its beak was a bright red flower. The veins in the leaves had a golden hue. The bird dropped the flower near Jason's hand, and then it looked from the flower to Jason several times. Jason, hoping he understood the odd behavior, picked up the flower. It was warm to the touch, as if the sun were shining directly on his fingers.

The blue jay began clicking its beak at Jason.

"Do you want me to eat it?" Jason felt very odd talking to a bird.

He assumed this was all brought on from the loss of blood and his death awaiting him across the clearing. He sighed and put the whole plant in his mouth and began chewing. The taste of honey covered his taste buds and instantly, the same warmth he felt in his hands filled his entire body. The pain from the open wounds stopped. He gritted his teeth and pulled the other two arrows from his legs but felt nothing as they broke out of the skin.

Jason swallowed the flower and adrenaline pumped instantly through his veins. The hunger and fatigue from the past days vanished. He felt more awake and alert than he could remember ever feeling in his life. He stood and noticed no more blood flowed out of him. He felt under his armor where the arrow had pierced his stomach. It was completely healed!

He reached behind him and unsheathed his sword. Standing up straight he glared as he pointed the sword at the army. This is what stood between him and Kristine now. Holding it in both hands, he ran straight toward them, feeling as if nothing could stop him from getting to her. The Orcs burst into laughter again at the foolish boy running at them.

When Jason reached the middle of the field, the forest behind him exploded with life. Thousands of animals poured from the darkness of the trees. Lions, deer, bears, wolfs, birds, bulls, and all other manner of beast and foul, led by a brown rabbit, ran fiercely at the army. The laughter of the Orcs died as they saw the mass coming at them. They began to draw their weapons. The animals had already overtaken Jason by the time the whole of the Orcish army realized what was happening. Before their eyes, the animals transformed in an instant. Suddenly the thousands of animals were massive creatures such as the Orcs had never seen.

The blue jay landed again in front of Jason.

"What are they?" Jason asked aloud.

"They are changelings called Othniel," Jason blinked in disbelief at Gaibian, who stood where the bird had landed seconds before.

Understanding flooded Jason's face as he realized Gaibian had been the blue jay.

"You just- But how did you-? Are you one-?" Jason struggled to get complete sentence out.

"I am not one of them," Gaibian laughed, "But I was trained in their amazing ability. Can we discuss this later? It looks like the battle is coming our way."

In an attempt to escape, many of the Orcs started running toward Jason and Gaibian, who stood alone in the field. The two raised their swords. Orcs began to circle around them. The Othniel had disappeared into the forest again, pursuing the majority of the army.

Gaibian and Jason fought back to back as the remaining Orcs tightened their circle. The two fought harder as Orcs began pouring in masses out of the surrounding forest. The fighting stopped, and the numbers around Jason and Gaibian continued to grow. They held their swords ready to fight and turned in circles, eyeing the army that surrounded them.

A mounted Orc moved through the mass as it parted to let him through. Another Orc walked beside him. Both were more heavily armored and decorated than the rest of the army. When they reached the middle, the mounted Orc jumped off the dark horse. The one that had been on the horse was clearly much older and carried more command.

"I always knew you would betray The Dark Lord, Gaibian," the older stood in front of the Elf and spat his words through a lisp, "Now drop your weapons!"

Jason immediately obeyed, Gaibian stood his ground.

"And I always knew you and your son would lead an army to its destruction, Grodan," Gaibian replied calmly, "After all, you are the ugliest Orc in the Dark Lord's army."

The rough green hand of Grodan slapped Gaibian hard across the face, "Your betrayal of The Dark Lord will not go unpunished, stupid Elf! I will take you to him myself, and perhaps he will grant me the honor of killing you!"

"It is unfortunate you will not live to see that day," Gaibian smiled, "You will die here by my hand.

Grodan laughed and put his face right next to Gaibian's, "I think not. Look around you. You are outnumbered and would die before your blade touched me."

"Look again, filthy Orc."

Grodan stepped back and looked around in fear. What had been his warriors had been replaced by the Othniel. Taking the opportunity, Gaibian raised his sword and swung around cutting off the head of Grodan. Grodan's son raised his weapon to strike at Gaibian. Jason had been too quick for him. He grabbed his sword and easily deflected the blow then buried his weapon in the Orc's belly.

"Nicely done, young prince," Gaibian patted Jason's back, "Seems you have gotten more training since we parted. Let us hope it is enough for what is to come." Gaibian raised his voice so all could hear, "And now we move on to Myrinas to end this once and for all!"

Jason looked at thousands of changelings around him then back at Gaibian, "I won't be going to Myrinas. At least, not yet. I can't explain why, but I have to go back to Ojai."

Gaibian nodded, "We will make sure you have safe passage there." Jason and Gaibian led the army back into the forest to the north.

*　　*　　*

Half the nation of Midlothian lined up to make the last leg of the journey to Myrinas. Jerech gave his final instructions to the council of the twelve. Afterward, they took their places, one to each of the twelve battalions; Jerech rode to the head.

"This," Jerech called out, "is a momentous day in the history of our people. On this day we reunite the broken ties with our human brethren. On this day we aid in the eradication of the vile Orcs that have infested this world. On this day we restore the peace that has been missing from our home. On this day we are free!"

Thousands of Elves cheered for their king. For a moment, even Jerech felt they could be victorious against their enemy. A dark cloud hung heavy over Myrinas out in the distance, and it was toward this cloud Jerech marched his army.

Tens of thousands of Orcs stood in wait. Ogres, intermixed with the army, towered overhead, loading catapults with boulders the size of a man, and covered in oil, ready to burn. At the rear, hundreds of arrows stood in front of archers with crossbows. By all odds, it seemed there would be no chance the forces of Silamond would fail. The dark army stood and waited without rest, each day increasing their lust for blood.

Two days after leaving Midlothian, Jerech's army arrived. They hid at the edge of the woods with the recruits of men they could convince to join from various villages along the way. Even with the additional support, the numbers did not amount to those of Silamond. It seemed that they were outnumbered ten to one.

The Elves peered through the trees, viewing the restless bloodthirsty army across the vast battle field. They all shared the same thought: This is our last stand. We die here today, or we die in our own land.

A horn sounded. Thousands of arrows launched from the trees. The army exploded out from the woods, running straight at their enemy without looking back.

15

Final Hope

Jason woke from a dreamless sleep feeling the cold stone beneath him. The months of training he endured with the Angels burned fresh in his mind; the difficult journey with Gaibian and the Othniel purged from his body. He slowly stood and looked around. Directly under him, the floor looked perfectly white, almost glowing. He turned and walked toward the throne. With each step he took, the ground grew back together; it seemed to be healing. His heart beat faster with each step toward the throne. He knew what he had to do to make it final.

The voice of his grandfather entered his mind, "Take the throne and breathe life back into the kingdom."

Jason ascended the steps. The jewels began to glow brightly on the large throne. What had only seconds before been a violent thunderstorm outside had turned to a calm, warm rain. Jason turned around and carefully lowered himself into the center of the throne. The entire room exploded with color and life. The once tattered throne room was completely whole as if it were new. Behind him, he could feel a tingle creeping up his back. Blinding pain shot through him like electricity as he felt his spine stretching and something growing out of his back. When the pain stopped, he reached back and felt the feathers of wings. The young prince bowed his head as the wings folded comfortably around him like a cloak.

The memory of Mount Angel, Oregon where he spent most his life, faded away. Dan and Carolyn England gone. Ireland gone. Jason held on as long as he could, but soon the beautiful dark-haired girl he loved began to fade slowly into blackness. Just like the other memories of his past, the love of his life, Kristine Simmons, was gone.

Once the growth was complete, he heard his mother voice in front of him, "It is done, my son. The kingdom of Ojai is in your hands. Now arise, Eraul of Angels."

In one swift motion, Jason stood and his wings burst open to their full span. He kneeled respectfully before Akarah's figure and held out his hands. She unsheathed the sword from Jason's back and placed it in his hands. The double-edged sword glowed white hot as the power of many generations of kings flowed through the Eraul's body.

"Now go, my son, it is time to finish this," with that Akarah's image vanished.

Jason walked toward the entrance to the magnificent throne room. All around, the city had come back to life. Water was flowing abundantly out of the large fountain in the center of the city. Jason stepped into the nearly dried-up river that came from the fountain and dropped off the cliff. The river rose up around Jason's feet. He followed it to the edge of the cliff, and looked down on the black clouds blanketing Myrinas. The endless flow of water dropped off the edge and burst through darkness majestically. Jason dove over the edge, and began to soar toward the ground behind the waterfall.

Half way down, Jason spread his wings and kicked off the rock wall, breaking through the waterfall. The world opened up around him, and he felt every soul beneath the black clouds below. The air flowed smoothly over his body as he spun around, parallel to the ground. Jason came to a complete stop where he knew a battle raged beneath and felt the warm sun on his back. He reached behind him and drew his sword.

With wings spread straight up, he allowed himself to free fall through the black clouds. A hole broke through the clouds with him as he carried the sunlight to the battle below. He landed hard in the middle of the fighting, causing the ground to shake slightly. He stood tall, facing the Elves and Men that fought side by side. His wings folded behind him.

Both sides had ceased fighting to stare at the figure. Jerech, who led the army, took a step forward when he noticed the Elvish features on the winged man. He felt a different shock than those around. The Elf king was not new to the race of Angels; however this particular Angel was more familiar to him than anyone but his wife.

"My son," he whispered.

Jason looked over at Jerech. His pale skin appeared even paler beneath his blonde hair. "Yes, father," Jason spoke directly to the king then turned and raised his voice, "I have come to put an end to this. Where is Silamond?"

Jerech stepped forward to stand next to his son and pointed toward Myrinas, "He is there, Jason. Inside the temple."

The dark creatures began to grow restless. Deep in the midst of Silamond's army an archer let loose an arrow. Less than an inch from the Elf king's heart the arrow stopped. Jason broke it apart in his hand and dropped it to the ground. All eyes stared at the Angel in amazement. Jason's eyes landed on the archer that had tried to kill his father. He flew straight forward, knocking down the Orcs that stood in his way, and cutting down many others with his sword. The movement was so swift the Orcish archer barely had time to react before a blade was buried deep in his belly. The whole of the Orc army had turned to stare at the Angel as he walked toward the city.

Deep inside, an old woman crept quietly through dark alleyways, directing the children out of the city through a hidden passage. When they had all passed, she noticed that two were missing. Her eyes searched franticly for them. After telling the children where to go, the old woman returned to the city, looking for the lost ones. It was oddly quiet. It seemed as if the fighting had stopped. When she came from the alleyway next to the temple, her heart wrenched with horror.

Two Ogres walked toward a larger one carrying the

two that were missing; two teenage girls, barely fifteen.

One of the Ogre's spoke to the larger, "Boardoc, sire, we bring gift. Girls tried to run, we catch."

Boardoc smiled wide, "Excellent, you have done well."

The girls were laid down in front of the Ogre. The old woman could not believe what she was seeing. "NO!!!!" she screamed. No longer was she an old woman, but once again the beautiful figure of the Oracle.

The two Ogres flew high in the air, turned upside-down, and landed on their heads, breaking their necks.

Boardoc stood, "The Dark Lord said you would come back. Best of all, he said I can have you when you did."

Kristine looked pleadingly at the teenage girls. Understanding what she wanted, the girls stood and ran away. Boardoc turned his head as the two ran away, then back to Kristine.

Anger filled the Ogre's eyes, "You just cost me a snack, you stupid little girl!"

With all her will, Kristine attempted to fight off the approaching Boardoc. Her fear paralyzed her. A bolt of light jumped out from Kristine's body, hitting Boardoc square in the chest knocking him back a little.

The Ogre laughed, "My turn."

He bent down and a large arm swung at Kristine, hitting her in the stomach. She flew back through the wall of a nearby house. The wind was knocked out of her when she hit. Pieces of debris fell on top of her, pinning her to the ground. She struggled to get free as Boardoc approached.

Boardoc eyed the Oracle hungrily. She looked up at him, trembling with fear. The Ogre was almost like she imagined from the stories she had read and heard. This one, in particular, stood just over eight feet tall. Markings were burned into his arms, chest, legs, and face. Varying tribal patterns ending mostly in sharp points. Sharp yellow teeth showed in Boardoc's evil smile. He licked his lips. The thing Kristine noticed most of all was that he was not fat, as she had always imagined ogres to be. Toned muscle covered the Ogre's body. He leaned over her and moved the debris off of her with ease. His face was nearly touching hers. She could see the red, hungry burning in his eyes, and she shuttered as he licked her neck and face. Despite the hot breath on her ear, Kristine felt very cold.

She tried feebly to recall the power she had used to help fight and to overcome Silamond the first time. It didn't seem to be enough. He had grown stronger but she still hadn't regained all her power. Silent tears streamed down her face as she thought first of the people that would die in this fight because she couldn't save them, then of the men that used to protect her, but were now gone. Her father died to keep her alive when she was young. Tanas watched over her like a brother, and tried teaching her all he could about this world and how to use her power until being killed by his father. Most importantly was Jason, the man she loved more than anything and watched die in her arms after he carried her all that way. She cried now, knowing she was powerless to stop this monster.

Boardoc moved his rough hand up Kristine's leg. She hit and scratched as his face. He laughed, and then slapped her across the face, leaving her feeling disoriented. The noise of the outside battle that had momentarily stopped, resumed once more; it seemed muffled to Kristine. She knew she wouldn't be killed, not yet. They wouldn't even allow her to kill herself, though that would be all she desired. Her body quivered, and she sobbed, thinking about the evil creature that would grow inside her. The Ogre gleefully licked the tears off her face and moved his lips to her ear as he untied the leather belt on his pants.

"I am going to enjoy you the most, pretty little girl," a low growl resonated in Boardoc's voice.

Slowly he lifted her dress to her waist enjoying every look of fear and disgust on the Oracle's face. Drool fell from the Ogre's open mouth onto her neck; she closed her eyes, trying to remove herself mentally from the scene.

Just as Boardoc was going to remove his pants, he was forcibly wrenched away from Kristine. A tall, winged figure stood in the opening, light shining around him. The sun had broken through the clouds and the cold rain was subsiding.

"Jason?" Kristine whispered hopefully.

"You're safe now, Saedin Oracle," Jason looked down at the Oracle, not showing a hint of recognition.

"Look out!" she screamed pointing at Boardoc. The Ogre had picked up his discarded swords and was now running full force at Jason.

"You cost me my treat, boy," he barked.

The swords swung down hard. Jason's wings folded around him, shielding the blow. Boardoc hit as hard as he could, unable to get through. The Angel's wings broke apart, throwing the massive Ogre backward. He landed on his back and lost hold of his swords. Jason flew up in the air and came down hard on the Ogre's chest as he tried to get back up. His head hit the stone, making him dizzy. He looked up at Jason as the Angel drew the sword from his back.

The amber in Jason's eyes seemed to burn as he glared at the evil creature, "Your days of raping women and killing the innocent are over. Return to the Seas of the Damned where you belong, spawn of darkness!"

Jason drove the sword easily in the Ogre's throat. Boardoc flinched and gasped for air, then fell, dead.

Several Ogres saw the fall of their leader and ran at the Angel. Kristine screamed when Jason was knocked to the ground by a club. The Ogres began kicking and punching him. Jason folded his wings around him. Spiked clubs rose and fell, hitting the wings hard. As he had with Boardoc, Jason broke open his wings, forcing the Ogres back. He stood, sword in hand. The Ogres charged but were killed, unable to land another blow on the swift Angel. More Ogres had been alerted and began to run at the Angel.

"Stop!" a sinister voice commanded from the stairs of the temple. The dark robes of Silamond billowed in a cold wind that flowed out of the temple. The Ogres shrank back in fear at the sight of their master.

Silamond frowned at Jason, "I thought your brother killed you."

"Didn't take," Jason replied, unruffled by the Dark Lord.

Silamond turned to Kristine, "It is so nice to see you back to your *young* self again. You make a dreadful old hag."

Kristine stood weakly, still shaking from her confrontation with the Boardoc. The Dark Lord stepped toward her.

Jason was instantly standing between them, "You will not touch the Oracle again. Your reign is finished, Silamond."

"No, my dear boy," Silamond stood an arm's length away, "my reign is only just beginning." Silamond reached out and touched Jason on the shoulder, his voice loud enough so only Jason could hear, "She'll go with me, and you will die."

Jason opened his mouth to answer, but before words could reach his lips, he was encased in a block of ice. Kristine screamed and ran toward him. The Dark Lord grabbed her and began dragging her toward the temple.

"You three, destroy this young fool." Silamond looked at the Ogres angrily, "The rest of you, go help the Orcs before our lines guarding the city are overcome."

All but the three largest Ogres ran to join the battle that sounded much closer than before. When the Ogres arrived, they found the renewed efforts of the Men and Elves had pushed back the dark army to the entrance of the city. With the help of the Ogres, the Orcs felt driven to fight harder. Elves and Men began to fall, and their army was now being pushed back away from the city. Jerech called for the lines to fall back to the trees. A horn sounded from among the Orc's ranks.

From out of the trees rushed an army of Orcs, led

by Gaibian. The Orcs inside the city let out a triumphant cheer. The lines of good froze in fear. They were completely surrounded.

"Spread out," Jerech commanded.

The order was shouted through the army, and reluctantly, they obeyed. The army began to spread itself wide as the hordes of Orcs closed in on both sides. Gaibian reached Jerech first, who had been standing directly in the middle, smiling at his comrade.

"Nice to see you finally arrived," Jerech grabbed the hand of his oldest friend.

"I had had to find some allies," Gaibian said, turning around at the approaching mass.

Toward the front of the Orcs, two elves, a dwarf and the only living Raltiiri were running.

"You two sure chose a bad time for a reunion," Dorian called to Jerech. "Mind picking this up another time? We have a war to fight."

"Let us end this," Raza said, agreeing with his friend.

The two drew their weapons followed by Arilie and Rioridan.

Jerech turned and yelled out to his army, "Turn around! We end this fight now."

The army showed greater hesitation but obeyed, still seeing the friendship of Jerech and the Elf that had an army at his back. As they readied the charge, the Orcs behind them ran through the gaps that had opened up in the ranks. They did not stop and fight Jerech's army, but continued on. Neither army could believe what they were seeing when the Orcs running toward Myrinas changed instantly before their eyes. Thousands of Othniel charged head first into the Dark Lord's army; followed closely by the army of elves led by Jerech.

*　*　*

The three Ogres surrounded the block of ice containing Jason. They raised their spiked clubs and swung at the same time. A burst of light exploded out from the center of the ice. It shattered, launching ice, and the Ogres, away from the Angel within. The Ogres enraged by the loss of their instant kill, stood and ran at Jason. He leapt into the air, and the Ogres collided head first into each other, falling to the ground. Jason landed in the middle of them. One by one, Jason threw them out away from the courtyard. The Angel gripped his sword tighter and walked inside the temple.

In the center of the entrance hall the Oracle stood in a block of ice up to her neck.

Her teeth chattered as she spoke, "Don't, Jason, it's a trap. Run."

From above, Silamond dropped hard on to Jason's shoulders forcing him to the ground. His head connected with the floor, cracking the marble on impact. Before Jason could recover, the Dark Lord kicked him in the ribs, causing Jason to fly up toward the ceiling. Silamond was now above Jason and hit him back to the ground. Debris flew everywhere as Jason's body connected with the marble floor once more. Kristine tried to scream through the cold, but nothing came out. She watched helplessly as the love of her life was repeatedly beaten.

"I've had enough fun with you, stupid bird," Silamond spit at Jason. He grabbed Jason around the neck and pushed him against a pillar. Chains of lightning crawled out of the Dark Lord's hand tying Jason in place. "I'm going to let you watch me drain the last of your precious Oracle's life and power before I kill you."

He drew a dagger from inside his robes and walked toward Kristine. He raised it up then stabbed down. The pang of metal on metal rang through the hall.

Jason's amber eyes burned at the Dark Lord, "You will not destroy another life."

With a flash of light, Jason forced the surprised Silamond back, and brought down his sword, cutting the Dark Lord in half.

The ice holding Kristine melted instantly and she collapsed, shivering on the ground. Jerech, followed by several men rushed into the temple. A cloak was wrapped around Kristine and she was helped to her feet. Everyone watched as the body of the Dark Lord melted into a puddle of water. They followed Jason as he walked from the temple. The black clouds that had shrouded Myrinas had completely cleared.

"He has defeated the Dark Lord," Jerech shouted, "He has saved us all."

Cheers exploded from every living soul present. Jason turned to Kristine, who was now being supported by

Gaibian. Jerech stepped next to them.

"Your people are safe, now," Jason said, "I must return home until I am needed again."

Jason spread his wings and flew up into the bright blue sky then out of sight.

*　*　*

Several weeks passed after the destruction of Silamond and the people of Myrinas watched their Angel savior fly away. Kristine did all she could to concentrate on helping the people rebuild the city once more, and to heal from those dark days. Her heart sank as she remembered the emptiness in Jason's eyes. She could not understand how he could not remember her after everything he had done to save her. It was then that she decided to climb to Ojai to find her answer.

The climb was easy for her. The draw to see Jason gave her power and strength she had never known. She marveled at the magnificent flora surrounding the walkways. It had been nothing like this when she was last here. The city was no longer in broken disarray.

Kristine walked through the doors of the palace that

stood slightly ajar. She saw Jason sitting in the throne with his eyes closed and wings folded around him. "The last time I was here the city was in pieces," her voice echoed through the large room.

"The city has healed itself," Jason sat unmoved, "As long as an Eraul claims the throne, the city will live."

Kristine's heart fluttered at the sound of his voice. She tried to keep her voice steady as sobs threatened to escape her throat, "You still don't know who I am, do you?"

She stepped closer

"You are Saedin, the Oracle of Myrinas."

Kristine's heart sunk. She stepped closer to the Angel, fighting harder to keep back the tears, "Yes, I am." -Her words were broken as the sobs began to break through- "I- I wanted to thank you for what you did for me and for the people of Myrinas. We owe you our lives."

"You owe nothing," Jason remained still, "It is the duty of the Angels to protect your people."

The silence after the echo of his voice felt final. Kristine turned and walked hurriedly to the doors.

"I dream of you, Oracle," Jason's voice stopped Kristine instantly.

She turned slowly and saw him standing directly in front of her. His white wings rested quietly behind him. His feet and chest were bare. Long white pants were tied snugly to his waist. Kristine's heart beat faster as she saw the magnificent beauty standing before her. She blushed as she felt herself crying openly.

"I dream about the day you saved me as well," her voice was only a whisper as she looked into Jason's amber eyes.

"That is not what I mean. I dream of a time before that, I think. We are both children. You call yourself by another name. We read strange stories to one another in a place I do not know. Can you tell me what these dreams are, Saedin Oracle?" The formal name pulled her slightly from her daze.

Her jaw dropped. She felt her entire body quivering and without realizing, her feet had left the ground. She now floated eye level with the Angel. Her body slowly inched closer to his. Kristine swallowed the lump that had formed in her throat.

Jason's eyes peered deep into hers as he waited expectantly for an answer. Her hands met with his warm, smooth chest. She felt his heart beating strong; the same heart she had felt stop almost a year before. Their faces were nearly touching, and in this moment she knew.

A whisper quieter than before broke from her throat, "You do remember."

Jason leaned forward, and his lips connected with Kristine's. Electricity flowed through their bodies as the world froze around them. Memories flooded back to Jason's mind. Daniel and Carolyn England. Mount Angel. Ireland. Keash Caves. His journey through a strange new land. And finally Kristine Simmons. Everything about the woman he loved and lived for opened up to him. His arms wrapped around her and pulled her body tightly to his. They pulled apart and their eyes met again.

"Kristine," his heart felt like it might explode from beating so hard, "I love you."

She smiled and tears of joy poured from her eyes, "I love you too Jason England."

They kissed again.

16

The Seventh Orb

The months seemed to fly by as Jason worked tirelessly, helping to rebuild Myrinas. The work progressed faster than anyone could have dreamed with the help of the Angel. In less time than imagined, the temple was completed. Just in time, too, as the day of the wedding had arrived. The entire city was bursting with excitement. A large feast was being prepared with the help of the newly allied Elves. Dorian worked with several of the craftsmen in town, creating a surprise firework display. This celebration meant so much more, since they would also be celebrating the defeat of the Dark Lord.

The women of the town were especially happy to assist in the wedding of their beloved oracle. They worked on bouquets of flowers to line the streets leading to the temple. Candles were placed in the fountain at the entrance of the city. The warmth of late summer air hung in the city through the night.

Jason opened his eyes and was glad to see the sun had not yet broken over the horizon. He got out of bed and walked to the edge of the cliff; he smiled as he looked over the sleeping city. All was peaceful as far as he could see. He flexed his wings several times and felt the rush of adrenaline surge through his body at the thought of flying through the air.

"Today is the day," he said quietly, the sun peaking up over the horizon. Jason felt the warmth of the sun start to cover him as he yelled, "Today, I marry Kristine Simmons!"

He leapt over the cliff head first, his wings folded against his back. The rush of cool air felt like a blanket around him. As the sun flooded the city, Jason spread his wings and soared over. Several children that had started out to the market with their mothers pointed at Jason overhead and tried to chase him. He smiled and waved.

Outside the city he saw fires being lit as the elves began preparing the feast for the many guests attending the celebration following the wedding. He landed in the center of the camp.

His father stepped out of the largest tent as Jason approached. "I am so proud of you, son," Jerech held Jason in a tight embrace, "I only wish your mother could be here."

"She isn't coming?"

"She can't. There are circumstances holding her back."

"I'm going to see her."

"Jason, don't! You'll be late."

But Jason didn't hear his father's words; he was already flying south to the Isles of the Dead.

Flying felt natural to Jason now as he soared just above the Black Forest, resisting the urge to dive, twist, and weave through trees. He had to hurry to find out why his mother wasn't coming. Jason pushed harder to cut through the air as fast as possible. He landed on the largest of the Isles of the Dead in just over an hour.

"Mother," he called out, "Where are you?"

Akarah walked calmly from a crowd nearby, "Jason, you

are getting married soon. What are you doing here?"

"Why aren't you coming to the wedding?" he demanded, "You aren't dead, you can still leave here."

"Jason," she looked sadly in his eyes, "I made some terrible mistakes. Promises were made so that I could keep you alive. I was trying to protect you. I am sorry, but I can never leave here again."

"I don't understand," anger left Jason's eyes and was replaced by pleading, "This is the most important day of my life. What could possibly keep you here? You're an Angel, like me. You're supposed free to roam the world."

"I am not free like you, Jason," she took her son's hand. "There is great darkness on Myriad far more powerful than Silamond. An evil that spawns the darkness here and it lies beneath the Seas…"

She was cut off as Jason passed her when he saw someone he recognized suddenly appear. Someone he knew should not be here. Ardel, the head of the Elders of Myrinas, appeared behind Akarah looking very surprised.

"What happened?" Ardel asked confusedly, looking directly at Jason.

Jason stepped around his mother, "Ardel, I'm afraid you're dead." Jason sighed.

Ardel looked even more perplexed, "But then why are you here? Did you die too?"

"No, Elder, I came to get my mother." – Jason turned to face Akarah – "I have to go let Kristine know so we can get father to officiate."

"Wait, Jason," Akarah grabbed his arm just as he was about to fly off, "I think we have someone better to help you."

She turned her son back toward the crowd of people that had now grown larger in numbers. In the midst of the crowd glowed a bright white light. The crowd parted as Jason was guided to the center. Jason could not believe his eyes when he saw the source of the light.

*　*　*

Kristine entered the doors of the chapel, holding her head high. Immediately, the whispers inside went dead. Everyone present stood and turned to face the beautiful bride. She took in deep breaths, too nervous to lift her eyes from the floor. Her heart told her to walk on, despite what she was told about the absent groom.

"He'll be here," she whispered to herself, "he has to be here."

She couldn't help herself; tears began to fall from her eyes and down her veiled face. Each step closer she felt her heart sink deeper into her stomach.

Still she repeated to herself, "He'll be here. He has to be here."

When she was half way down the aisle, the doors burst open and a rush of warm air swept through the building. The congregation gasped. Their eyes followed the gust of wind, as did Kristine's. High above the room, a magnificent Angel, dressed in silky white pants and a matching tunic, slowly descended until he landed next to the bride. Jason smiled widely, tears of his own falling down his cheeks. Tears of overwhelming joy.

Kristine was momentarily frozen in place, not knowing what to do. All etiquette fell from her. She ran down the aisle and threw her arms around Jason, "I knew you'd come. I knew you'd come."

"I wouldn't miss this for anything, love."

When they separated, it suddenly became apparent the elder Ardel wasn't there.

Kristine looked up into Jason's amber eyes, "where's Ardel?"

Jason's smile broadened, "He's gone, sweetie."

"What do mean? Why are you smiling? This isn't funny! Maybe your father should marry us."

Whispers were growing louder behind the couple.

Jerech turned to Gaibian, "Go find the elder."

Gaibian stood and exited the temple; before the doors closed he had changed into a blue jay and taken flight straight toward Ardel's home.

He landed and knocked hard on the door, "Hello? Is anyone home?" No answer came. "Ardel, its Gaibian. Everyone is ready for the wedding to start; we need you there."

Still no answer came. Gaibian opened the door, walked in and continued calling Ardel's name. Upon reaching the bedroom Gaibian found him in his bed. Slowly, he approached the still figure. Ardel wasn't breathing.

Gaibian opened a window and jumped, changing as he did. He flew as fast as he could to the temple and in through a high window in the chapel. He flew straight down and changed back before landing next to the marital alter.

He leaned in and whispered to Jason and Kristine, "Ardel is dead."

"I know," Jason smiled, "everything is going to be fine. Sit down Gaibian."

"What do you mean? The head of the Elders is dead. He is supposed to officiate. How is everyth-"

Before Gaibian finished, a bright light shown down from above. All eyes looked up except for Jason. His eyes remained locked on his bride. Six glowing blue orbs circled slowly around an even brighter white orb in the center as they descended toward the alter. When they reached it, the six blue orbs formed an arch over the alter and the white began to glow brighter. All other light in the chapel lost definition. Everyone but Jason was frozen in awe. As the brightness began to diminish, the shape of a man could be seen inside of the light.

Once again, whispers began as the man became more defined. Gaibian looked back and forth from the man to Jason.

The light settled and a familiar face stood before them, smiling.

Kristine looked up into the loving eyes of Jason, "You knew. This whole time, you knew."

The audience was speechless.

Gaibian swallowed hard, "But you died."

"Please have a seat, Gaibian," the prophet Tanas's voice sent a wave of peace over the room. Gaibian took his seat next to Jerech.

Jason and Kristine knelt down behind the alter, their backs facing the audience. At the gesture from Tanas, the two joined hands and looked lovingly at each other. Tanas placed his hands on top of theirs.

"Through eons, many stories of enduring love have existed. They have been told and retold. This is one of those stories. Never, since the day they met, have these two drifted in their affections for each other. Even upon the day this wonderful Oracle was chosen, the memory of her existence wiped from her world, did they drift. The flame of their love is so pure and eternal nothing, not even the ancient magic of Myriad, could extinguish it. So it is, to my great pleasure, that I shall bind their love to last forever more. Jason, you will repeat after me."

Jason repeated the words told to him, "It is to you, Kristine Simmons, that I give my heart, my soul, my life from this day and for eternity."

Similarly, Kristine repeated the words from Tanas, "It is to you, Jason England, that I give my heart, my soul, my life from this day and for eternity."

Tanas gestured for the couple to stand. As they did, Liza, Jason's grandmother, stood behind Kristine. Jerech stood behind his son. Jason and Kristine were handed the white gold bands. At the same time, they slipped the band on to the other's left ring finger.

As they did this, they again repeated the words from Tanas, "With this token we are bound."

"You may now kiss your bride," Tanas said to Jason.

Jason lifted the veil from Kristine's face. The two took each other's hands, leaned in, and kissed the first of many kisses they would share as a married couple. A great cheer rang through the city of Myrinas.

Epilogue

The yellow cab rolled up in front of the house Jason had left over ten years ago. Jason handed the driver a generous tip. "Wait here," he said. He climbed out of the car and shut the door behind him.

Before he had made it half way up the walk way Carolyn England had already thrown the door open and ran out to hug her adopted son, tears in her eyes. "Oh Jason, I knew you were still alive. I can't believe it is really you," She hugged him tight, afraid it was just a dream.

"Hi," he paused and kissed her on top of the head. "Mom, I didn't come alone."

Jason looked back to the cab. The passenger side door opened. Feet appeared under the door followed by a long skirt dropping down to the ankles. A woman's head appeared over the door, her dark hair blowing in her face.

Carolyn let out an audible gasp. Waves of memory washed back into Carolyn's mind. A beautiful, little dark haired girl, with piercing emerald eyes. The sweetest smile, the purest heart, the best friend of her adopted son.

When the woman brushed the hair from her face, there was no doubting who she was. Jason steadied his mother who nearly fell over from the shock.

"Daniel!" Carolyn could only think to call her husband's name.

Her tears were flowing freely now. Daniel England rushed to the door, thinking his wife was in trouble, but froze when he saw his son. He dropped a glass and the towel he had been using to dry it off. The glass shattered when it hit the ground. At the same time, the same flood of memories of a little girl rushed back to Daniel's mind. He began walking slowly toward Jason. Jason smiled and opened his arms. The much shorter Mr. and Mrs. England were wrapped Jason's arms, both crying at the joy of seeing their son. The woman remained at the car, silently watching the family reunion and feeling the joy emanating from them.

Jason pulled back and turned, "Aren't you going to say hello to Kristine, too?"

Kristine stepped toward Jason, whose hand was stretched out to her. "Hello Mr. and Mrs. England," Kristine smiled at them both, "It has been a long time."

Daniel acknowledged her for the first time and adjusted his glasses, "My Lord how you've grown!"

Kristine blushed.

"And please call me Dan," he added quickly.

"You really have grown into a beautiful woman," Carolyn said, taking Kristine's free hand as Kristine turned slightly pinker. Carolyn's eyes went big, "And it seems perhaps you should be calling us mom and dad." Carolyn turned to her son, "I know it's been a long time, Jason, but this does seem the sort of thing you could have at least called about. We did raise you, after all." It was difficult for Carolyn to be stern when she felt so elated.

"Well," Jason began, but was quickly interrupted from a voice inside the cab that still sat idly in the street.

"Mom, can we come out yet?" a blond haired boy with amber eyes that matched Jason's poked his head around the open door, "I really have to pee, and Alexander keeps poking me."

"It isn't like that, mom," a dark haired boy with emerald eyes like Kristine's, but otherwise looking just like the other boy, popped his head out from the other side of the cab, "Michael keeps invading my space. I just want him to stop."

Carolyn's jaw dropped, and her husband and son had to steady her again. Jason tried not to laugh.

Kristine smacked Jason's chest and turned sternly to the boys, "You two stop fighting, or you'll be separated. Do you understand?"

Both boys chorused with, "Yes, mother."

"Now come out here say hello to your grandparents," Kristine said with the gentleness of a mother.

The boys jumped happily from the car and ran to Carolyn and Daniel.

"Well I'm sure you've figure out from the lack of proper introductions, these are your grandsons," Jason tried to act as if this was a common occurrence, "Our twin boys Alexander and Michael."

"Clearly you have a lot to explain, son," Daniel said as he hugged Alexander.

Kristine looked at her husband, "Perhaps we should go inside."

Jason nodded, paid the cab driver who had graciously unloaded their luggage, and then he followed his parents into their home.

Once inside, the adults seated themselves in the living room while the twin boys took it upon themselves to explore the house.

"Well, the short version," Jason said, "is that I found Kristine about a month after I left home. After a little over a year, and some minor obstacles," -Kristine laughed at her husband's choice of words - "we were married. Eight years ago, the twins were born."

The boys' loud footsteps could be heard above them.

Kristine touched her stomach, "And about three months ago, we found out I was pregnant with another."

Mr. and Mrs. England sat in silence, trying to process everything that had happened, when the twins ran into the room.

"We're hungry," Alexander said.

Michael followed with, "Yeah, when can we eat?"

A grandfather clock chimed six times.

"It is time for supper," Carolyn said.

All four adults stood up. Kristine walked over to her mother-in-law, "I would love to help."

"Wonderful," Carolyn smiled, "Maybe you can tell me the long version while you do."

While they sat to dinner, Jason and Kristine recalled their time together; with some minor details excluded for the time being.

*   *   *

In the deepest crevasse of Seas of the Damned a figure sat in the shadows staring into a basin watching the family enjoy their meal. He stretched forth a clawed finger, dipped it into the bowl and began to stir the water.

"Kaelthith," two voices spoke together. One cold and commanding. The other pained and sorrowful. Both seemed weak as if being used for the first time.

The waters inside the stone bowl became still and the Daedra, Kaelthith, appeared inside. He knelt down as if in prayer, "You summoned me my master?"

"Silamond has failed me," the cold voice grew stronger, "It seems that your old enemies have returned." Red eyes glowed in the darkness.

"What would you have me do?" Kaelthith's revere had instantly turned to malice.

Out of the shadows, the demon's face leaned close to the basin. Sharp spikes covered the hairless head. Grey skin stretched taught on the skeletal face and a white goatee hung from his chin. Hatred burned in the sunken red eyes. Through gritted teeth he hissed, "It is time you returned to Earth and showed them what happens to those who oppose me!"

A wicked grin crept up Kaelthith's face, "So it shall be done, master Draedin."

Raltiiri

The Raltiiri are a peaceful race, who are known to live for centuries among the great trees in which they build their cities. They spend their time hunting and gathering in the forests, some trading with other races in nearby kingdoms where they are welcome. Their wooden cities are built like fortresses, yet are hidden from the untrained eye. It is ideal for them to protect themselves from predators and enemies.

They are seen walking on all four limbs, though it is not unheard of for them to ambulate bipedally. The Raltiiri body is eight feet long, not including the prehensile tail. The ten foot long tail is able to wield one-handed weapons, or so legend says. Their golden brown fur covers them from head to tail, only the bottoms of their three-fingered hands and two-toed feet uncovered. The face appears cat like, with the males having wild, untamed hair growing like a mane.

After the early Raltiiri found the forests in which they wished to build their cities, they found allies in the Elves. They were given great weapons and armor and took the role of Protectors of the Wood. A small group of them traveled across the sea and settled in a forest of red trees. As a means of protecting themselves, their creators allowed them to evolve dark red fur.

Peaceful centuries passed, before an enemy revealed themselves. It was unknown to Men and Elves and Dwarves how their Raltiiri friends would react to full-scale invasion, but all soon learned that the Raltiiri were among the most vicious fighters alive. The invasion was over within days.

Most of the Raltiiri leaders encouraged peace, but some troop warriors sought blood openly. Eventually, the world went to war, and every Raltiiri was hunted down save one. One last Knight...

Acknowledgements

It is humbling when you finally reach the end of an adventure to realize all those who made the journey possible. Without those people, I am sure that I would have never reached the end.

I want to start by saying thank you my wife Mary. She was persistent in reading my first draft even though it was very messy and disorganized. Those first editorial notes from her were a big step forward. She has also been very supportive of me through this endeavor and has helped me to unscramble my thoughts to get them in the story, as well as helping me to not lose hope when I would get discouraged.

Next I want to thank my —Stalker! (you know you are) for the many years she has put up with cliff-hangers without resolutions; for the many middle-of-the-night emails with new material and changes, and for staying so excited about this book and the forth-coming stories in the series. I also thank her for helping me to come up with the names for Daniel and Carolyn England. After all, where would Jason be without his adoptive parents?

What is a good book without a good editor? Kara Barney Kettle has been a fantastic help with her editorial expertise. She has helped take Myriad to fantastic new heights with her in-depth notes. Her excitement and willingness to help brought new vigor to completing this project and helped me get started on the next. Regardless of the busy schedule she maintains in her personal and professional life, she has always found the time to take another pass through the story for me.

Through the many years it has taken me to get this story onto paper, I have grown fond of each of its characters and gotten to know their emotions well. However, some experiences are difficult to recreate with real and believable emotion without having been there yourself. Thanks to my mother-in-law Katie, I was able to bring even more tangible emotions into the story in ways that only a mother could have. I appreciate her time in reading it and in the hours spent giving me her notes and suggestions.

That being said, I wouldn't be here or who I am today without my own mother Valerie. She has always given me her love and support ever since I found my love for writing. It was, I admit, entertaining to watch her fall in love with the characters and her reaction to the seemingly insurmountable obstacles placed in their path.

This story has brought about what I feel are some great new characters and races. I have had friends and family share those feelings with me as well. One such race is the Raltiiri, for which the credit goes to one of my best friends Daniel Adams. I appreciate the time we have had to discuss our various stories with one another, as well as the opportunity we both have had to bounce ideas off of one another. I look forward to the time when he has completed his first book and to see his many talents properly recognized.

I have had many friends and family members offer to read the unfinished work and give me their insights, and appreciate their willingness to try. Though not all have had the time to be able to do so, I would like to express my appreciation for them as well as those who were able to find time in their busy lives. Angela Cook for her notes towards the final stages of the book. My sister-in-law Laurie, for reading it early on and sharing her thoughts, as well as getting my brother Jeremy to read it. My sister-in-law Kelli Shimek for her thoughts and ideas while reading the story. And of course I want to say thank you to Zak Salisbury, Catie Fessler, Cassie Lowe (my big-little sister), my cousin Angela (though she did begin to read it), and any others I may have missed who wanted to read it but were unable to find the time.

Lastly, I want to thank those who have patiently waited for me to complete this first book and to be able to finally read the story I have often mentioned. It has been helpful to have the regular inquiries as to when they could finally read my book. Each and every one of you have made this journey possible and all the more worthwhile. Thank you all for sharing it with me. I hope you have all enjoyed it and will encourage everyone you know to read it as well. Never, EVER stop reading!

James is an autistic author, husband, and father of 3. He initially started writing because he loves telling stories. More than that, writing became a way for him to communicate more clearly and express his innermost thoughts and feelings. He has an active imagination and likes being able to put it to practical use. Writing and reading help him to center himself, make more sense of this crazy world, and decompress all the noise of life. He wants to share his stories with the world so he can help someone the same way others' stories have helped him feel seen and like he wasn't alone. Naturally he also enjoys spending time with my family and playing games with his girls.